Facebook... James Eagle Feather

Youtube... Eagle Feather Empire

IG... Eagle Feather Empire

Twitter... @EmpireFeather

Linked In... Eagle Feather Empire

Whatsapp... Eagle Feather Empire

www.eaglefeatherempire.com

THE LOST MAYAN

EAGLE FEATHER

THE LOST MAYAN

iUniverse books may be ordered through booksellers or by contacting:

iUniverse
1663 Liberty Drive
Bloomington, IN 47403
www.iuniverse.com
844-349-9409

ISBN: 978-1-6632-1424-9 (sc)
ISBN: 978-1-6632-1425-6 (e)

Print information available on the last page.

iUniverse rev. date: 12/17/2020

Her heart pounded wildly in her chest as she fell to the wet grass. The cold air burned like fire in her lungs as she struggled to catch her breath. Her eyes darted around the surrounding prairie... seeking desperately for a place for concealment.

In the distance she heard the war cries of the pursuing Crow... the hooves of their horses thumping heavily against the cold ground.

Her stamina was giving out fast. Yet... through sheer terror she willed herself to her feet. The sticky blood that coated her hands and arms was matted with loose grass and mud. She stumbled forward aimlessly... wanting nothing more than to escape... wanting nothing more than to survive.

In the dead of night, she planned her escape. Her captures, the Crow, had bound her arms and ankles. She labored tirelessly throughout the night until finally, her hands were free. Just before the rising of the sun there was stirring within the Crow's camp. So she knew the time had come to make her move... or else suffer helplessly at whatever fate awaits her.

After she freed her legs she reached for a large rock... the only weapon at her disposal. She crept slowly upon her dozing watcher and raised the stone above her head with both hands. With every last ounce of her frail being, she brought the stone down. The force of the impact shattered both rock and skull as the warrior's soul was jarred from his body. Instant death of the warrior gave little comfort to the woman as she raised pieces of shattered stone above her head. Driven by fear and bitter anger she delivered another blow to the soft wetness that was once a man's skull. The blood spraying like a fine mist on her arms and hands. Because of this act of self-preservation, the woman knew that a fate far worse than death awaits her if she were to fall into the hands of the vengeful Crow.

The early morning sun slowly made its way above the horizon... bathing the land in soft golden colors. In desperation, she prayed to the rising sun... her breath fogging the air in front of her. Her weary legs trying to gather strength to move... but she stumbled with every step she made until she finally felled.

The Crow quickly covered the distance upon great and powerful horses. The warriors knew they were encroaching upon Lakota territory... completely disregarding all treaties that were sworn by the two opposing tribes. But with lust and vengeance in their wicked hearts... nothing less than the life of the woman could quench their feral blood-lust.

They soon discovered the woman and quickly surrounded her with their horses. They let their war cries fill the morning air as their horses formed a moving ring around her... slowly moving inward... slowly closing the moving circle... drawing it tighter and tighter. Her frenzied eyes darted from face to face. To the Crow, she looked like a beast seeking desperately for a gap within the closing ring. Soon all possible means of escape were cut off by the whooping Crow. Completely exhausted, the woman dropped to her knees... all hope slowly draining from her tired body.

A warrior dismounted a moving horse and pounced on the woman. In vain the woman fought against him... but she was too weak. The circling horses and the war cries dazed and confused her... the flying mud and grass only added to the chaos. The warrior struck her with his lance. Agonizing pain shot through her drained body as she crumbled to the ground. Unconsciousness threatened to take hold as she struggled to clear her vision. Another wave of pain washed over her as the warrior drove his foot deep into her side... her breath driven from her lungs. The man lifted his lance above his head and brought it down on the woman... she gasped as she felt the pain like molting fire through her color bone and neck. The war cries and pounding hooves were replaced by a high pitch whine... a whine that came from her head. She fell to the ground... beaten... broken... defeated. All she could do was close her eyes and wait for the final blow. The blow that will lead her to the cold embrace of death.

But the darkness of death never came.

Through the pain she forced her eyes open... only to find her attacker lying in the soft grass beside her. She forced her eyes to focus... more out of fear than curiosity. His eyes were open... but there was nothing there... no recognition... no intelligence... the eternal flame had been extinguished as they gazed unseeingly towards the heavens.

From the edge of her view, her peripheral vision had caught the movement of dancing shadows and moving light. She saw horses and their riders moving swiftly away from her. She tried focusing her eyes. Slowly she looked up before her... and there stood a great horse... dancing back and forth... eager to join the chase. On its back sat a man... a man unlike her captors. His buck-skinned clothe were completely different... and upon his head were five large feathers fanned out. The early morning sunlight shimmering from off the eagle feathers... turning them iridescent.

Slowly... dauntingly her eyes scanned her surroundings. In the distance, she could see her captors being chased by men dressed similarly to the one that stood before her. Her paranoid mind wanting to believe she was now safe... but bitter experience had thought her to prepare to fight. But she had no fight left in her. Her escape and morning of running had drained her... and she had no energy left to defend herself.

The man dismounted and stepped to her. He was a Lakota... a warrior of a thousand mortal combats. But what he saw in the woman's eyes reached far beyond the hardness of a lifetime of war... far beyond his harden outer shell... and touched his heart with an icy finger. The panic... the fear... the helplessness... all etched in her eyes. Eyes that were wild… tired… but still they reached out to him pleadingly. Then she spoke. It was a language he had never heard before, despite the fact he had sat in on council meetings from many different tribes. Confused, he simply stared down upon her. Her eyes became unfocused as she spoke in that strange language again. Her voice was soft… filled with pain. Again she spoke… then her eyes rolled to the back of her head and consciousness seeped from her body.

The man knelt beside the woman… her tattered clothes and arms were covered in wet grass and drying blood. The very sight caused his hardened heart to soften. He knew he had to help her… he knew this in his heart. But little did he know… in that strange language… she had pleaded for that very thing. And the last thing she said before succumbing to the dark realm of unconsciousness was "Please, don't hurt me, for I can take no more."

"What you've heard is true, we killed two Crow," Tall-Eagle said without preamble as he entered the lodge of a tribal elder. The elder, In-The-Woods, sat towards the back of his tipi… in his hands, he held a long-stemmed pipe. From the stem hung three golden eagle feathers. When In-The-Woods didn't respond, Tall-Eagle continued. "It was they who entered our lands to do harm to a caretaker. It was they who broke the peace, not I."

In-The-Woods slowly and methodically began to pack the bowl of the pipe with tobacco. The thin elk-hide illuminated the interior of the lodge with sunlight. Even from within, one could easily see the winter counts brightly painted on the outside of the tipi. The lodge was typical… towards the back laid plush furs spread out upon the ground. Towards the front were bundles of traveling gear. To the left of the door were hunting equipment… hunting bows and flint tools for on the spot preparations. To the right laid his weapons of war. Although he was considered an elder, In-The-Woods still had a hankering for warfare.

His many years on the battlefield is what had given him the respect needed to be a tribal leader... and one day, chief.

The two sat quietly... awaiting the arrival of others. Soon there was a quick shaking of the door flaps... then the flaps parted and elders and warriors both entered the lodge. Without speaking, each man found a spot in the lodge... forming a wide circle. Each man sat with their legs crossed with somber expressions.

In-The-Woods lifted the pipe into the air... offering it to the seven directions of the Lakota spirits. He then held it high above his head and said, "Oh Great-Spirit, we offer this tobacco to you... so that our words may be true... and your wisdom may be heard." From the men, there were scattered "A-ho" as they slowly nodded their heads in agreement. And from the small fire pit he withdrew a small burning ember and placed it within the large bowl of the pipe. Slowly he inhaled... the ember growing brightly as small crackling sounds came from within the bowl. Small tendrils of smoke drifted lazily from the bowl as bellows of smoke rolled between his lips. Again he slowly inhaled then quickly raised the pipe above his head then passed it to the man sitting to his left. Although a total of 19 men filled the lodge, all sitting tightly packed in a tight circle, there was an eerie silence. Only the occasional "All my Relations" could be heard being whispered into the heavens.

Each man had their turn smoking from the pipe... their prayers being made in the silence and stillness of their hearts. After the pipe made a full circle, ending at In-The-Woods, the elder held the pipe close to his heart. His eyes closed tightly as his lips moved slightly... praying in a tone just below the threshold of audibility. Slowly he opened his eyes and allowed them to silently run over each man that sat before him. He was sure that each knew exactly why they were summoned. He also knew that each one was fully aware that the future of the tribe would be determined here and now... at this very gathering.

"Brothers, hear me," In-The-Woods stated slowly. "It has come to my attention that today treaties were broken. And as a result, two Crow are now dead. Tall-Eagle and a small hunting party were seeking small game when the cries of a woman caught their attention. They arrived to find a Crow beating this woman. So Tall-Eagle did what he felt was right, putting an arrow in his back, piercing his heart. The Crow then fled back beyond our boundaries. But don't be mistaken, brothers, they will return."

In-The-Woods then passed the pipe to the left, the person holding the pipe was the only person permitted to speak. But nobody wanted to say a word until they heard the words of Tall-Eagle. Shortly the pipe reached him and he held it tightly. "It is true, my brothers and I came across a Crow, a coward, fighting a woman... a care-taker. The woman was injured, bloody. I followed my heart and I do not regret this. If it leads to war, I will fight alone. May my blood be the start of a new treaty."

Although the words spoken by Tall-Eagle were true, he knew such bravery was without merit... for each man knew that these so-called treaties with the Crow were constantly shifting at best. These far-from-friendly peace treaties were constantly being tested, pushed and stretched beyond its limit. Not by the Lakota... but by the Crow. And if war was to truly ensue... each Lakota warrior was far beyond prepared.

Tall-Eagle passed the pipe... but no one spoke. Finally, it reached In-The-Woods. As is custom... once the pipe had made a full circle, the floor was then open for all... one no longer needed to possess the pipe in order to speak.

In-The-Woods sat in deep thought... a kind of thought that came with the wisdom of long experience. The reason for these uneasy treaties with their many enemies was done for a simple reason... the Little-Star-Band was a small band that valued its anonymity and isolation far beyond anything else. "War will be made," he said in a strangely docile tone as he nodded his head ever so slightly. "The question is, how long will it last? How many will fall?"

"Only I should fall," Tall-Eagle said with strength of conviction. "It is I who made war," he said in another empty gesture.

"Why should Tall-Eagle be the only one permitted to fight the Crow?" Left-Wing spoke. "Have I not provided well for the tribe? Let me fight them with Tall-Eagle. I deserve such glory as well," he spoke with a wolfish grin on his face... his mind abound with the glories of war.

In-The-Woods made a noncommittal sound as he looked over Left-Wing... the tribe's finest warrior.

"Two Lakota warriors against the entire Crow Camp, how is that a fair fight? Unless Left-Wing fights without weapons," another warrior said. There were quick laughs and chuckles among the circle. But the laughter quickly died as In-The-Woods leveled an icy stare at Blue-Leaf... the one who had made the joke.

"Tell me about this stranger who you are willing to die for," In-The-Woods said to Tall-Eagle.

Tall-Eagle thought of the woman... her strange look... the strange language she spoke... even her hair... its color and texture was completely unknown to him. "She is a care-taker,' he pointed out inarguably. The Lakota had long ago constructed a complex social order for its people... and had given each a name. An adolescent had to go through three stages before it became an adult. Because a child's earliest years is its most impressionable time... for males, the first seven winters are spent with his mother... where matters of the heart are taught and learned. That child is called, according to the social structure "Tomorrow." With his mother, he learns compassion... love... patience... to become loving and gentle. During this time a child learns the very essence of life and what it takes to grow strong and prosperous as a whole. Because of a woman's role... she is known as the care-takers-of-tomorrow.

The following seven winters are to be spent with the father, where he learns to hunt... to endure pain.... to fight and to provide for the whole. But the very root of these actions must lay in what was taught by the mother. Then after the seven winters with his father... he is then handed over to a spiritual advisor where he is taught the ancient knowledge and wisdom of a People. It is here the child truly learns to become a man... to connect all that he had learned up until this point... to understand the sacredness of the circle and the delicacy of the web of life.

"She is a care-taker," Tall-Eagle repeated... this time somberly.

"She is not from this land, but I don't think she is an invader," Blue-Stalk said openly. "Her skin is that of the rising sun, like the color of leaves in the winter's chill. It is not dark like ours. Nor is it pale like those of the invaders. Nor is it the color of those who came before them... yellow like those of the setting sun or black like those of the rising sun."

"But her hair is like theirs," Blue-Leaf said. "Or more like that of a buffalo's tail." Again the group chuckled. All but Tall-Eagle.

"Yes, her hair is strange. I have never seen the likes. It's curly... long and different shades of brown. And wild." Tall-Eagle stated.

"You have yet to fully answer my question," In-The-Woods stated.

"She is in White-Sun's lodge. She is tending to her wounds. I have yet to speak to the stranger for life had drained from her and hasn't returned," Tall-Eagle said. "But I saw into her heart. Her eyes. They plead... cried out for help, and so I will help," he said in a feeble attempt to answer the question.

"They will ask for her return. And perhaps the blood of another to reimburses that of their fallen brother," In-The-Woods said. "But in the event they seek only her return?" he asked Tall-Eagle... already knowing the answer.

"I will take her place," Tall-Eagle responded.

"So either way, it is war," In-The-Woods said.

Darkness plagued her dreams. Pain... like light... fighting away the darkness that envelopes her weary soul. Oh, how she longed for darkness. Eternal darkness. Her soul... ablaze with fire as it drifted through the pain of light. Above her... she feels an evil spiritual presence. Unseen and unsubtle. But it is there... she feels it... like a heat above her. In a silent scream she cries out in agony. But the sounds were mere whispers. She prayed to the ancient gods for peace... for guidance... to help her escape the network of pain that she finds herself entwined in. She prays to the ancient gods for darkness. Eternal darkness.

Tall-Eagle entered the lodge of White-Sun. Her tipi had an extra hide thrown over it... so the interior was laid in darkness. He moved towards the back. White-Sun sat on the ground beside the stranger. Tall-Eagle took his place beside her and gazed upon the strange woman. A very strange woman indeed. He slowly evaluated her with slow, steady eyes. White-Sun had washed away the blood and soot and did her very best to comb her strange curly hair. He could tell the woman was lost... drifting in an aimless, yet healing sleep. Her face had become pale and drawn. Every so often she would wince and bare her teeth in pain. Small beads of sweat trickled down the side of her face... plastering her hair to the side of her face.

Tall-Eagle reached a hand out to brush away the wet hair from her face. Under his touch he could feel the heat radiating from her head. Yet... her weary body would shiver with cold chills.

"This woman is ugly," White-Sun said completely unexpectantly. Tall-Eagle had to tear his gaze from the magnetic force of the stranger's being. He looked at White-Sun puzzled.

"She is not," he said simply.

"Look at her mouth. Her upper teeth protrude from her narrow face. Her bottom teeth aren't far behind. She looks like a deer. A sick deer. Perhaps she is sick. Have you ever seen the likes of her?" she asked Tall-Eagle. His silence answered her question. "So she isn't from around her. Perhaps she brought the plague with her from the east, from the lands of the conquering white man. You know plague and death precede their arrival. Perhaps you have brought death to our people."

Tall-Eagle didn't respond to White-Sun's accusation. Instead, he laid a finger very gently against the side of the stranger's face. To himself, he grinned slightly. "She does, perhaps, resemble a deer." He traced his fingers down the side of her narrow face and tiny chin. She did have an extreme over-bite on her narrow face... giving it a protruding look. But to Tall-Eagle... it was a narrow elegance far from "ugly."

Again she winced in pain. But Tall-Eagle felt utterly helpless as this stranger laid in dark and troubled dreams.

"The blood wasn't hers," White-Sun said, breaking his concentration.

"She has plenty of small cuts and bruises. Perhaps after a little rest she can take her leave," she ended bluntly.

"Perhaps," Tall-Eagle said softly. As he looked down upon the sleeping woman... again he gently swept away the growing beads of sweat. And with this touch... he felt as if something soft... yet euphoric was being drawn out from deep within his soul.

From outside the tipi there was a commotion. And then a shrilling war-cry pierced the afternoon silence... shattering his deep concentration. As Tall-Eagle exited the lodge he heard the whining of a horse. In his mind he saw many Crow swarming the camp... their wicked hearts and minds bent on vengeful bloodlust. But what he found was a single Crow warrior. He sat upon a horse that moved its head from left to right... its hooves beating the ground in nervous stomping.

The Crow let out another war cry as he brazenly rode closer to the camp. His demeanor bolstering self-confidence... his clothing was that of war attire. His beaded breastplate was the color of blood. His face was painted in black and red and from his Mohawk hung a single feather. His shield bared the symbol of two red lines that swayed. In one hand he held a spear... in the other he held not only the reins which guided the horse but a single arrow as well. Yet his bow remained slung across his shoulder.

The Crow drew even closer to the camp. The Lakota warriors had arrows fitted in their bows... all aimed at the intruder.

"Where is the stranger?!" the Crow yelled... using the common Dakota language of the Great Plains. "She murdered my brother! Bring her to me!" he snarled furiously as the horse pranced back and forth... bobbing its head up and down.

"It was I who killed him," Tall-Eagle said as he stepped forward. The rider drew even closer... glaring at Tall-Eagle from atop his horse.

"I take it this is yours, Brave-One," he said as he threw the arrow he had onto the ground before Tall-Eagle. Tall-Eagle recognized the feathered arrow at once. "I retrieved it from the back of a warrior, Brave-One." His emphasis on the name made it abundantly clear he had no respect for him. This angered Tall-Eagle as he fought to control his rising fury. "But, no, that one was not my brother," the Crow said.

"The stranger murdered my brother as he slept. Just like this Brave-One murdered my friend while his back was turned. Ha! Mighty *Sioux* warriors!" The use of the derogatory term was deliberate as he tested the patience of the men before him.

"The woman stays," In-The-Woods stated as he stepped forward... standing beside Tall-Eagle. "She is on our land. She is our guest. You expect us to abandon our guest and deliver her to torment and death?"

"You shelter murderers? Cowards? Tell me something, Old-One-With-The-Brave-Heart, are you willing to risk the lives of everyone in this camp... for a stranger?" the Crow inquired he grinned nastily. "Return her to me so that punishment may be induced. And I assure you, I have no intention of killing her. Give her to me and our treaties will endure."

"It was you who broke the treaty," In-The-Woods said, meeting his gaze.

"'It was you who broke the treaty,'" the Crow mimicked. "Return her to me," he repeated as he pulled the horse even closer and staring down at him imperiously. The many warriors refitted their arrows... pulling even tighter on the strings. "Return her or it shall be open war."

"You Crow, want war with the Lakota?" Tall-Eagle said in a voice deepened by strained anger.

"Not just the Crow, oh Brave-One." Again his voice was heavy with sarcasm. "As we speak our scouts are scarring the Great Plains all the way to the Great Mountains. Where they will gather your enemies. The Comanche. The Shoshone. The Utes. And many of our allies. We will wipe you from this earth, Brave-One. You and your people will be forgotten in history. All we want, the Old and Brave-One, is what is rightfully ours. Our laws dictate her fate."

"These are not your lands. Your laws hold no sway," In-The-Woods said fitting the Crow with a glare leaden with defiance.

The Crow's lips drew back in an animalistic snarl. "So they speak for you all!" the Crow shouted as he paced his horse back and forth again. "So be it, *Sioux!* It will be war! I am Red-River and I have spoken!" Pride echoing in his voice. With this being said he raised his spear high above his head and let out a shrilling war-cry. A cry so loud, it spooked the horse he rode... causing the mare to rear up. The Crow then turned and in a full gallop rode in the direction of which he came.

The warriors with the bows loosened the tension on the string. In-The-Woods was very impressed with their discipline.

"It seems war has found us," he said as the warriors gathered around him.

They all, including Tall-Eagle knew their own hearts... and their skills with bow and arrows on horseback. They knew they could easily defeat the Crow. However, none had the illusion about their ability to stand against so many. The Shoshone alone was a great and formidable foe. They are clever... cunning... very dangerous and completely without mercy. With this thought alone Tall-Eagle felt his stomach tighten in a spasm of dreadful anxiety. *What will become of our children?* He thought to himself as his mind was gripped by cold dread.

"War has found us, indeed," Blue-Leaf stated. "An evil choice is before you, In-The-Woods. The stranger or..." In the silence and unfinished sentence, Tall-Eagle knew the pain of Blue-Leaf's heart. "I will stand by my brother of war, Tall-Eagle," he said, echoing Tall-Eagle's thoughts.

In-The-Woods said nothing. Instead, he turned his gaze towards the west... as if hoping to spot an answer that would guide him in their perplexities. None was found. "Aside from the Crow, our enemies dwell many miles from here. To reach their camp is at least a moon's journey," he stated slowly... deliberately keeping his voice in a neutral tone. "Our allies, the Nakotas, the Dakotas, and the Cheyenne are but two hands journey."

"Enemies of the Crow are likely to be friends of the Lakota," Blue-Leaf stated hopefully.

"Perhaps," In-The-Woods said softly. Treaties and alliances among the various tribes were complex and often elegant affairs. Affairs that would take many trips and tokens... something that took time to adequately prepare for. And time is something they did not have.

"We have many powerful horses," Tall-Eagle said. "We have enough to send the women and children before us, out of harm's way. They could reach the Oglala's by the rise of the full moon."

"And I, along with a few warriors will go with them to defend against the Crow. You need but a few warriors for them," Left-Wing stated.

Again, In-The-Woods grew silent, taking in every word that was spoken.

Abruptly, Left-Wing started to laugh. "The cowards! Did he not sound brave as he spoke to us? We should have shot him off his horse."

"To kill a man without justification is not the Lakota way," In-The-Woods answered. "Despite what was said or how poisonous the words, he was but a single rider who made no aggressive move towards any of us."

"Do you think they would have shown us the same courtesy?" Left-Wing said.

"And do you not call them cowards?" In-The-Woods stated simply. "Let us not lose track of what is important. Tall-Eagle has given a wise solution. With the horses bearing a heavy burden and moving at a swift speed, the women and children could reach the Oglala village in a hands time. Whereas were we all to move as one, it would take us over twice that amount of time. Let our decision be a wise one."

"I see no decision," the one called Yellow-Horse said. "Even if we were to fall by the hands of our enemies, at least our names will live on. Let us send our future before us."

From the gathering men, there were sounds of agreement. In-The-Woods had no doubt that trouble lays at hand. Perhaps a few skirmishes between the Little-Star-Band and the Crow. But for the most part, he knew that his people would be safe, for the Crow and their alliances were no match for the mighty Nations of the Lakota. With this thought, his mind became at ease. "Prepare the horses." At the command, both New-Calf and Standing-Bull moved with a spirited quickness to retrieve the two finest horses. "Red-Bear and Charging-Elk shall prepare to ride." With this being said, the two warriors left to gather what was needed for such a strenuous journey.

Within the tribe... each member knew and understood their responsibilities... and they executed these duties with great pride and honor. The Little-Star-Band had many horses. And these horses were cared for by a group of young braves. Before long New-Calf and Standing-Bull... two of the horse watchers, approached with the two fastest horses the band as a whole possessed. One of the horses belonged to Tall-Eagle.

Upon seeing his horse being led by Standing-Bull, Tall-Eagle smiled mischievously to himself... for he knew his horse was very spirited... and extremely selective of who he would allow to ride him.

Tall-Eagle turned his gaze towards the afternoon skies. He found he had to squint against the bright and burning sky... for the clouds overhead was torn and drifting lazily towards the east... offering no protection against its rays. Spring, the season of resurrection, was such a beautiful time of the year. He loved how the sleeping prairie came to life in an orderly procession. From the trees and grass to the brush and wildflowers... each growing and changing in color as the season progresses.

Like many of his people... he would often take a moment each day simply to feel the warm sensation of the sun bathing his face. To breathe deeply... filling his lungs with the sweet smell of Mother Earth. To enjoy the sweet fragrance of wild flowers in bloom as they drift upon a gentle breeze. Or simply listen to the hushing sounds as the wind softly swishes the prairie grass from side to side. Or to listen to the songs of birds or other wildlife of which the Great Plains provides a safe haven for.

Each season brought with it it's own sites and beauty... it's own sounds and scents that would permeate a soul and bring a complete joy and appreciation for life. But still, his favorite was spring.

So in the stillness of his heart... he silently said a prayer... thanking the Great-Spirit for this day.

At that moment... his horse stepped forward... lowering its proud head to gently nuzzle the neck of Tall-Eagle... breaking his train of thought. Tall-Eagle smiled as he reached back to pat the magnificent creature on its powerful neck. The horse bobbed its regal head up and down at the loving gesture. "Soon you will have the fate of our people upon your back," he said as the horse let out a loud neigh and pranced before him. "I do not doubt that you will do us proud."

"Indeed, he will," In-The-Woods stated as he too patted the horse. "Never have I seen such a horse."

Tall-Eagle removed one of the five feathers from his hair and braided the feather into the horse's mane. "Remember my friend," he whispered to the horse, "you are Strong-Spirit, the swiftest of the swift. And remember that you now wear something that once soared above the clouds... something that once touched the heavens."

"Is Strong-Spirit the reason you have yet to take another wife?" Left-Wing said, jokingly in bad taste.

The wife of Tall-Eagle, Girl-Lost, had crossed over to the Land-Of-The-Spirits many winters ago. Girl-Lost was heavy with child when she had fallen ill... and when she crossed over she had taken their child with her. For a time after the loss, the mighty warrior felt like nothing more than a mere shadow of his true self. A dark shadow of a man inhabiting a shadow world. In time the pain began to lessen and he was able to smile again. But the pain was still there... deep within his heart... where he carried the bittersweet memories of Girl-Lost and the family that should have been his.

Tall-Eagle said nothing at the comment... but his facial features clearly indicated the raw anger boiling beneath the surface.

But just beneath the anger... In-The-Woods saw a flicker of sadness... and knew instantly the two raw emotions was a volatile mixture. "War is before us," he said... trying to defuse the situation. "Let us not darken our hearts by things that cannot be undone. Instead, let us remember a bow with even the smallest crack cannot hold up in a time of war."

"This is true. And who's bow is mightier than Tall-Eagles'?" Left-Wing said by way of an apology.

Again, Tall-Eagle said nothing... instead he continued to pet his prized horse... doing all he could to subdue the rising anger.

Left-Wing was a good friend to Tall-Eagle. They both had fought side by side on the battlefield... each one depending on the other for survival. The test of time and the constant balance of both victories and defeats had brought them closer and closer together with each passing battle. But even so... the topic of Girl-Lost was like a wound that will never fully heal. A wound that laid directly over his heart and the slightest exertion will lay it exposed and vulnerable… oozing and seeping with pain.

"A bow is only as mighty as the one who wields it," Tall-Eagle said… although he tried to subdue the pain and anger, there was a hard and angry edge to his voice when he spoke.

"This is true as well," Left-Wing replied trying to inject a humorous tone… hoping the moment had passed. But again, Tall-Eagle said nothing.

Left-Wing had an effective physical presence… an air about him that spoke of confidence. His long black hair was parted in the middle and braided on each side. Within his braids were eagle plumes and two eagle feathers, which hung loosely down his back and rested between his shoulder blades. Despite the chill of the wind… he wore only a bright red loin clothe and a red and black beaded choker. He still held his bow and arrow in hand from the Red-River encounter.

Before long, Red-Bear and Charging-Elk arrived. The two warriors wore buckskinned over shirts and leggings that shimmered with brightly dyed porcupine quills. Their moccasins were decoratively beaded with the colors of the seven directions. They carried in their sashes tomahawks, flint knives, lances with a bow swung over their shoulders and a quiver full of arrows on their backs. They also carried leather pouches full of pemmican and dried berry cakes to eat on their journey.

Upon their arrival, Red-Bear grinned gleefully at the sight of Strong-Spirit. "Finally my time has come," the big warrior said as he stroked the horse's neck.

Again, Tall-Eagle began to smile, mischievously. "You seem happy," he said cryptically.

Then the moment became serious. "My relatives," In-The-Woods said to the two messengers. "This is perhaps the single most ennobling pursuit ever undertaken by the two of you." The acting chief spoke slow and methodically… never breaking eye contact. "With the speed of an arrow… ride to the people of Oglala and relay this message. 'To the warriors of the Oglala, tell this to the Wolf-Maiden, open war with the Crow and their allies lies before Her. Amass Her young warriors and prepare them for battle... for our enemies will greatly outnumber the people of the Little-Star-Band. The Crow, they wish to spread their reign of terror... to lay waste to the Lakota for we choose to give sanction to a Care-taker. One of which they accuse of murder. So long as she is in our care, my warriors will protect the sanctity of life and those who produce it. People of the Hunkpapa, the Crow are amassing enemies of the Sioux, with the intent of destroying us all. Join our ranks, Brave warriors, so that we may put an end to the Crow and their story."

When In-The-Woods had finished... the two messengers fully repeated the message in turn... both parroting In-The-Woods every word. The old man slowly nodded his head. "Then bring the warriors along the Folding-Left-Path, for we will be taking this path as well, and we shall meet along the way." He then took a step towards the two. "May the Great-Spirit journey with you," he replied in a tone he felt was grave enough to convey the seriousness of the journey.

"A-ho," Red-Bear said. Tall-Eagle held Strong-Spirit until Red-Bear was atop... but the moment Tall-Eagle released the great horse, he thrust suddenly forward and the big man was almost unseated. Tall-Eagle knew that would happen... and for a moment he was eager to witness it. But now the atmosphere had become too real... too grim as reality started to settle in.

"Whooo, Strong-Spirit!" Red-Bear soothes as he clung desperately to the horse's mane. The big horse wildly tossed its head and let out a shrilling neigh. His tail flicked back and forth as it eagerly pulled against the leather bit. And then it reared up onto its hind legs... prancing as it bucked its head. "Whooo, whoo," Red-Bear whispered as he bent over the horse's arched neck... all to no avail.

"You cannot ride Strong-Spirit," Tall-Eagle said to Red-Bear as a ghost of a grin played on his lips. "The name 'Strong-Spirit' was not given in fancy idle. Either he carries you or he doesn't." He then stepped forward and ran his hand gently across the creature's neck while he spoke directly to the horse. "Strong-Spirit cannot be controlled. But he will lead you to victory, always."

Suddenly the horse halted... its ears quivering... flickering forward then backward. Again it let out a neigh... but this time it was more calming. But Red-Bear could still feel the horse's muscles twitching eagerly beneath him. But at the same time... he felt connected to the powerful beast.

Charging-Elk was already atop his horse... the two started in the direction the sun sets. Strong-Spirit became eager to follow... willing to take Red-Bear to his destination.

"Safe journey, my friend," Tall-Eagle said to Strong-Spirit... and then lashed the flank of his faithful horse. With a sudden burst of raw power... Red-Bear felt the mighty horse's eager assent as it launched forward.

The warriors and In-The-Woods watched as the two messengers went forth... riding as swiftly as the wind. They watched as the two passed from sight... disappearing over the rolling hills of the prairie.

Tall-Eagle then turned to In-The-Woods. The acting chief stood gazing off in the direction of his messengers with a look of concern on his brow. His long hair was streaked with gray... but the old warhorse stood as erect as the young warriors that surrounded him. And unlike these same warriors... he had but a single eagle plume tied into his bread.

"The outline of a plan had been made," Tall-Eagle stated. "In the morning our women and children and elders are to set out for the village of the Oglala People. No doubt we will hold council when the sun began to set so that we may detail this plan. But until then, what shall we do? Already the warriors grow restless. And then women and children will sense this."

In-The-Woods said nothing. He continued to stare out towards the east... biting on his lower lip as if deep in thought. He could sense that there was an atmosphere of apprehension that now lingered over the campsite. An atmosphere that seemed like a dark and oppressive cloud that seemed to hang over the Little-Star-Band. Silently he became angry. The peace and stability of his people had been shattered... and the sense of tranquility seemed irretrievable.

In-The-Woods eyed each of the warriors around him. Tall-Eagle was right... the men were indeed restless... and the acting-chief did not want his warriors to harm themselves in their growing fury. He then thought of the women of his band. Women who would never speak their fears aloud... but instead become somewhat hostile in their own anxiousness. He then thought of the rest of the male population... most of them have not seen very many winters... they are too young to engage in war. And the rest have seen too many winters... their age prevents them from wielding weapons.

Finally, In-The-Woods said... "Today we smoke as much buffalo meat as we can carry. For tonight... we celebrate, for our hunt has indeed been a good one."

His statement had caused the warriors to mutter among themselves... for they didn't see the wisdom in his decision. But the acting chief was wise and calculating by nature. The decision he made was out of necessity... for he was trying to create an illusion that would preserve a safe haven for his people for that night... in turn providing a safe escape for those who couldn't partake in the upcoming war.

Despite the confusion... the warriors would do as instructed without question. So each warrior departed in turn... returning to their own lodge to tell their families of the celebration that will take place. Tall-Eagle had no surviving family... he was alone in this world. So he stood still... remaining by the acting chief's side.

In-The-Woods summoned Standing-Bull and New-Calf, the two horse-watchers that were present. "Retrieve Two-Braids and Spotted-Feather, then be sure the horses are well fed and watered. Then, using only your minds, I want you to divide the horses into two groups. One group should be of warhorses, those that have speed and perform well in battle. The other group will be workhorses, those that are powerful and can endure great strain. Now, go."

With quick steps, the two went to find the other two horse-watchers. Before long only In-The-Woods and Tall-Eagle remained.

"When the band is divided, you will assume command of the warriors," In-The-Woods stated.

"Of this, I am aware," Tall-Eagle responded.

"Are you prepared for what lies ahead?"

"Can one truly be prepared to take the lives of others in their hands?" Tall-Eagle said.

"You speak with your heart and your heart speaks in truth, Tall-Eagle, my boy. The mighty warrior who prefers peace for the sake of his people. This is how I know you are ready."

"Which warriors will stay behind?" Tall-Eagle asked the chief.

"That is a question for tonight. A question for the council. For now, we prepare for celebration." After saying this... In-The-Woods began walking towards his lodge... a large tipi that was well painted with dream symbols.

Standing alone, Tall-Eagle looked about the campsite, where he saw people going about their business... preparing to tan the buffalo hides from their successful hunt. Women were carrying buffalo hides to the small creek that lay just east of the site. As custom... these hides will be soaked in the mud by the creek for seven suns. Doing so will loosen the hair and could easily be scraped away using the rib of an elk. Within the campsite were poles where people were smoking long, thin strips of buffalo meat. Some of this meat was being dried in the sun while others were being cured over smoking fires.

They were in the Moon-Of-The-Red-Grass-Appearing... so mayflowers were just begging to bloom. Children of the Little-Star-Band were scattered over the prairie... gathering as many as they could in their small hands. Others were gathering a variety of berries... eating some as they went... for they had grown tired of eating dried berry cake and dried corn. Each fall... when the trees and the land take on their beautiful farewell colors... they would travel to the place where the people grew wild corn. There they would trade with them... then dry the corn for winter eating. And each year... upon breaking winter's cocoon... the children would anxiously hunt for serviceberries, chokeberries..., wild berries, or buffalo berries... anything sweet. Their hunt would be in vain for the berries were still tart and sour.

As he thought of the children... now laughing and running about the prairie... his heart bled for them all... for in their confusion they are always the innocent victims of any war. But this was the singular most tragic aspect of war that he emphatically disapproved of... waging war against a tribe who would murder the innocent in the same fashion as warriors.

Tall-Eagle was no doubt a seasoned warrior who had fought countless battles. The warrior prided himself on the bold and courageous wars he had waged against Sioux enemies... which were many for the Great Sioux Nation made adversaries all too easily. But a war waged against the capable is honorable. But to kill for the sheer pleasure of death and destruction... where innocent casualties greatly outweigh the fighting warriors... this is cowardly beyond reproach. And the Crow would not hesitate to murder children.

Tall-Eagle again turned his attention to the camp. The center of the makeshift campsite was a large open space where dance ceremonies were held. Here there would be drumming, singing, and laughter. But on this solemn day... the round center lay quiet and still despite the measured success of the spring hunt. There was no laughter or music... for their future a whole was all too grim for celebration. He wondered if there would be joy and laughter that night... for celebration must be held.

Aimlessly, Tall-Eagle began to wonder about the campsite... lending a helping hand here and there as he went. Before long he found himself standing outside the lodge of White-Sun, he began to wonder rather his heart and soul was being drawn to this place as if on some spiritual level... or rather it was simply done subconsciously? Either way... he felt joyful for being there... and he wanted to check on the stranger anyway.

Tall-Eagle shook the flap of the buffalo hide door... announcing his presence. White-Sun allowed him to entered, and he found the woman preparing to make a small fire within the center of the lodge. He said nothing as she took small embers and placed them in the hole dug for the fireplace. Upon these glowing coals, she places dry grass and small twigs. Before long, the embers became a small living flame.

"Can one ever truly understand the spirit of fire?" White-Sun asked as she placed a flat stone within the flames. "Does fire not provide life and light? Does it not provide warmth and comfort? Tell me, Tall-Eagle, why would the Creator of all things create something that gives life so much joy and comfort, yet can take life in the most painful and horrific way?"

Tall-Eagle stood in stunned silence... wondering where such a line of questioning would come from. He knew the woman was speaking about the dreadful prairie wildfires... something that kills animal and plant life and human life indiscriminately. Something that killed with flames that traveled as fast as the wind that fed them. Although they happened yearly... only once in his thirty winters has he witnessed the actual golden serpents that hissed with tongues of fire.... Withering through the dry prairie grass... destroying everything in its dreadful path.

"Why do you ask these things?" Tall-Eagle inquired.

"The spirit of fire is in us all," she whispered cryptic with calculating wisdom. "What feeds the flame within you, Tall-Eagle?"

Tall-Eagle studied her a moment from across the small fire... trying to understand the cryptic wisdom in her words. White-Sun came from a family of great warriors and spiritual leaders. She now travels with a young helper by the name of Mocking-Bird. Both White-Sun and Mocking-Bird were loved by all for their kindness and their desire to help. As the Little-Star-Band pursued the buffalo herds across the Great Plains, the two had become the tribe's healers. Using roots and herbs to cure various illnesses... medicines that were prepared by Lakota Medicine Men, for White-Sun has yet to become a recognized Medicine Woman. She believed it was all in due time.

"My flame perished with Girl-Lost and our child," Tall-Eagle said finally.

"This is not true, for the fire of your People is strong, for the love of your people is strong." She then retrieved some bird eggs and cracked them over the flat stone within the fire. Upon contact, the eggs began to crackle and hiss. Another perk of spring is that prairie bird eggs could be found in abundance... and they are served as a special dish.

"How is the stranger?" Tall-Eagle asked... denoting his real intent for the visit.

"Conscious has yet to return," she said sharply, speaking the obvious.

Tall-Eagle looked back to where she laid... but all he saw was the plush buffalo blanket that embraced her. "How long will she sleep?" he finally asked.

In response, White-Sun's dark eyes twinkled with an almost

ominous mischief-like quality... something completely outside the realm of her character.

"Why are you so concerned with this Deer-Lady?" White-Sun asked.

"Deer-Lady?"

"Yes, Deer-Lady. Does she not have the appearance of a sick deer? Thin and frail? I told you she might have brought the plague with her."

Tall-Eagle did not respond... for he was wisely choosing his battles. "The Deer-Lady," he said softly.

"This will be her name. And I will choose another when the time comes," White-Sun stated almost defiantly.

"Will she not be capable of choosing her own name?" he asked.

"Is it not custom of the Sioux women to decide the fate of woman captives? To choose rather they are enslaved or embraced as one of us, or set free to return to their own home? Is this not our custom?" she asked.

"Indeed, this is our custom. However, the Deer-Lady is not our captive. She is MY guest," he said, putting heavy emphasis on "My."

White-Sun slightly shrugged her shoulders then smiled with eyes that reflected the light of the fire. She then went back to attending her eggs.

With undisguised admiration... Tall-Eagle stepped closer to where the Deer-Lady slept. The buffalo robe was pulled high on the woman's chest... the fur was slick with sweat. The Deer-Lady's face was dripping with perspiration... causing her strange curly hair to become plastered to her forehead.

Tall-Eagle looked at her long, sweeping neck... watching as the light of the fire turned her golden flesh pale. Sweat pooled at the hollow base of her neck... slowly he dabbed it away with soft leather. With the soft light of the small fire playing upon her narrow face... the Deer-Lady seemed so unexpectedly beautiful to him. So beautiful that he could not pull his eyes from her.

"Does she not look sick?" White-Sun asked.

With effort, he managed to pull himself away from the seductive beauty of this woman. "What do you have against the Deer-Lady?"

"Am I not fulfilling my obligation as both a care-taker and a healer?"

she asked inarguably... and then a deep silence crept stealthily between the two. And once again he found himself being lost in her beauty.

Outside the tipi was the sound of a drum. Tall-Eagle knew they were testing the elk-hide drum for the night's celebration. "Will you and Mocking-Bird partake in tonight's festivities?" he asked White-Sun.

"The young one and I both will be there in turn. But somebody must stay with the Deer-Lady. I have seen where simple sleep had become death. We will not let this happen to the Deer-Lady."

By this time White-Sun had begun to eat her eggs... remembering to set aside a small portion in honor of those who came before her. Again the drums sounded outside the lodge... and he knew that soon council would be held in the lodge of In-The-Woods.

At that moment, Mocking-Bird entered. In her arms, she carries small branches for White-Sun's fire. "There is still a chill in the air," she said to Tall-Eagle as if answering a question. Mocking-Bird seldom spoke... but Tall-Eagle didn't think much of it.

"I will see you at council," he said to White-Sun then stepped out into the spring air.

The sun had made its way towards the west... where it sent back long yellow fingers that reached between the clouds to touch the ground. These yellow beams of sun-light danced in the prairie grass... and the wind played in it as well... causing it to bellow and ripple like flowing waves.

In the center of the campsite, young men were placing firewood into piles. Their feathered headbands and decorated war shirts marked their rank within the tribe. There were a few young women preparing food... wild rice, beans, rose berries, buffalo stew, elk steak, and fry bread made with goose grease, just to name a few. But even they were dressed for the occasion... wearing knee-length skirts and leggings made with the softest of deerskin. Their moccasins and skirts were embroiled with brightly colored beads. Their waist-length hair was bound in red leather. As they went about their work, the young maidens spoke of the great warrior they dreamt of one-day marrying. Indeed, Left-Wing was a name that came up often.

Tall-Eagle slowly made his way to the lodge of In-The-Woods. The bottom of his lodge was rolled up all around its entire circumference... rolled up to about waist-high. Here is where the council will be held... and now a cool breeze could flow freely within the interior of the lodge.

Again the large drum began to sound... sending out loud echoes rolling across the prairie. The sound of the drum reverberated throughout his body... and he knew then that despite the grim circumstances... tonight's celebration will become a joyous one.

From atop of a heavily forested hill... Red-River stood with his back braced against a tree. The afternoon sun had come and gone... and now it was sinking behind the western hills. Growing shadows reached out with long, embracing arms from the east... covering all the land in darkness. And under the cover of this darkness... he will be able to move closer to his Lakota enemies. From this limited vantage point... far atop of a ridge... he was learning very little about his enemies. So he needed to be closer.

Throughout the day he watched the Lakota campsite... watching as they went about as if no threat had been issued by the Crow. Red-River foamed with silent fury. The arrogance of these snakes in the grass only added to his fury. He believed he possessed the powerful spirit of the war gods. A spirit that gifted him with a wolf's innate ability to spread fear and terror... and to kill by striking the jugular of his enemies. *Yet my enemies prepare to celebrate?*

From behind, another Crow scout crept stealthily towards Red-River. Making his way through the thick, twisted, and bare limbs of trees that had been stripped by the harsh breath of the winter's spirit. Small buds were swelling on each branch... but the forest seemed bare. The scout's name is Black-Feather. Through the trees, Black-Feather could see the light of the Lakota fire burning on top of the hill. The steady pound of a drum floating on the air... competing with the buzz of nocturnal insects that filled the small forest of trees. "Soon the sun will be gone," Black-Feather said as he stood beside Red-River. "Before the moon make's its appearance we should move closer."

Red-River said nothing as he stared at his companion... but his dark eyes glittered fiercely in the last rays of the sun. A steady silence grew between them as they kept their eyes on the Lakota campsite... listening to the voices of the night and the beat of a drum.

Black-Feather swatted at a mosquito that fed on his arm. And in the gathering darkness, Red-River scowled at him. The spring season was a time for hunting. And according to Crow law... warriors and hunters were forbidden to use salt... for not only do they attract mosquitoes... but it causes an odor in their sweat as well. An odor that will scare away the game they are hunting.

Black-Father's eyes visibly narrowed at Red-River's silent rebuke. But still... they remained silent. Under any other circumstance, the two would have snapped at each other like rabid dogs.

The sun was now gone... and under the first shadows of the night, they made their way towards the Lakota. They knew Lakota scouts would be on full alert... so the Crow's every move had to be slow and calculated. Like an evil shadow, they passed out into the night... staying low and their eyes constantly shifting. Soon, the ominously dark skies will hold half a moon. But even half a moon provides enough light to see an intruder.

The two Crow boldly crept on their stomachs to the campsite. They got so close they could hear the laughter and talking of some women. A man then lit the fire in the center of the campsite. The small flame grew in intensity. And soon flames were reaching up high into the heavens... banishing the darkness of the night. A single cry from a singer set the drummers in motion. The drums, no doubt, marked the begging of the celebration.

The two Crow watched as the Lakota girls rose to their feet. And with their arms folded, they began to dance slowly around the fire... shuffling through the grass on beautifully beaded moccasins. The slow temple of the drum was soon followed by the cry of singers. The two entities blending into each other... creating a soothing melody that sent ripples through the Crow's souls.

The two were impressed.

But even so... they were here for a purpose. To gather as much information as they possibly could... information that could aid in their downfall. Red-River couldn't help but smile sadistically to himself. Privately... in the deepest... most secret recesses of his heart... he didn't want war with the Lakota. Nor was he pained over the death of his brother. Instead... he wanted Bull's Tail... the woman who murdered his brother. And not for the sake of vengeance either. But he needed to continue with the ruse. For doing so... according to Crow Law... with the help of the entire tribe, they would pursue and track her down to the far reaches of the planet... hunting her like a wild animal in order to exact their own particular brand of vengeance. And to get Bull's Tail... Red-River was determined to remove any and all obstacles that stood in his way... including the Lakota.

Red-River literally shook his head, as if to clear it of these thoughts. They were not only deep into enemy territory... they were also alone and within reach of a tribe they had threatened to exterminate. So he needed to stay focused.

The Lakota girls grew more spirited in their dancing as the drum's temple sped up. Before long they were spinning in elaborate circles with their arms out-stretched.... laughing and singing as they did so. The two admired the way their decorative dresses fluttered and cast a dancing silhouette against the fire as they pranced around the inner circle. And at the call of another singer, the men began to dance as well. With every move they made, there was a soft rattling sound. Their claw bracelets and necklaces, and porcupine quill decorated war shirts added to the beautiful array of sounds. Their feathered headdresses shimmering with the slightest of head movement. The long fringe on their leggings fluttering with their every step. But had Red-River or Black-Feather been paying attention... they would have realized that every man present was beyond their fighting years.

Tall-Eagle sat amongst the men and women within the lodge of In-The-Woods. Council had yet to begin... so they all sat in silent stillness... each one wrapped in their own thoughts. But Tall-Eagle listened to the sound of the celebration taking place. Closing his eyes... lost in the euphony of singing and drumming.

Within his mind, he saw himself standing outside the dancing circle... watching as the symphony of clattering shells and porcupine quills beckoned to his opened spirit. And in the midst of this celebration... he sees the Deer-Lady. Her strange, curly hair flowed free... cascading back from her narrow face... down her slender shoulders... the light of the fire causing her to glow.

She too was watching the dancers... her arms folded in front of her as if to stave off the chill of the spring night.

He goes to her.

She sees him... and holds his stare for a moment.

But he had to look away.

But still, she stares.

He becomes uncomfortable... but fights against it.

He steps closer... and holds open his buffalo robe... boldly embracing the two of them beneath it. And there... in his dreams he holds her.

"Relatives," In-The-Woods said... completely shattering Tall-Eagle's daydream... bringing him back to a dark reality where he had to face what must be done. "Tonight we hold council," In-The-Woods continued, "So that you all may know what is to take place. Some of you are aware that Red-Bear and Charging-Elk have been sent to the Oglala Nation for reinforcements. But it may be many suns before they arrive, and the number of our enemies is unknown." The elder stopped... allowing his words to etch themselves on the hearts of those who sat before him. He wanted every detail of his plan to be thoroughly understood.

In-The-Woods explained how he knew the Crow would be watching the campsite... confused about the celebration taking place. Due to this celebration, they will be misled to believe the Lakota's are staying... unaffected by the Crow's threats. In the morning... Tall-Eagle and

Left-Wing will lead a small band of warriors to launch a surprise attack on the Crows. The Lakota warriors are to first scatter the Crow horses and set fire to their lodges. And they will stay at the Crow's site... launching wave after wave of attacks. By doing so... they will be buying time for In-The-Woods and Bright-Arrow, who will be leading the women, children, and elders to a place of safety.

In-The-Woods made it absolutely clear that no one is to take down their tipis... for after the Lakota warriors are done with the Crow... they are to return to this very campsite and pretend that all the women and children and elders are still there. And the longer they can hold this ruse... the more distance In-The-Woods could place between their people and harm.

Tall-Eagle slowly nodded his head to the words of the acting chief. Without a doubt, In-The-Woods' knowledge was deep... and his tactics and strategies of war were very subtle... creating superb illusions to deceive and confuse their enemies. But rarely do things go according to plan. "Your words are wise," he said to the acting chief. "But the telling of a plan is far easier than carrying it out."

"I fear that your heart speaks the truth, my young friend," In-The-Woods said. "But the words I have spoken are mere strategies and strategies only. Strategy is not victory. For this, we must fight."

There were low murmurs among the group as some nodded their heads in agreement. At the prospect of war... Left-Wing's face was ablaze with excitement. "Are we to choose which warriors will stay and fight and who will escort the band?" he asked the elder. Tall-Eagle knew Left-Wing was speaking of his cousin, Blue-Leaf.

Blue-Leaf was new to the Warrior Society. He was still young... therefore possessed an erratic impulse to constantly try to impress the seasoned warriors. His eagerness to count coup had placed himself in many dangerous situations... but Left-Wing was always there to save him. Even now he asks so that he may protect him from himself.

"The Crow are a ruthless people," In-The-Woods said to Left-Wing. "They pride themselves on moral decadency. Such an inferior race will take great pleasure in slaughtering children... let alone a very young warrior."

"What you say is true," Left-Wing said agreeing. "Do you recall many winters ago you asked me to help the council figure out the hearts of the Crow? They are indeed brutal, primitive. But that is a weakness, not a strength. They fight with themselves. Their pronounced lack of discipline creates constant internal chaos. They are like prairie birds, wild chickens. Hostile? Yes. But dangerous? Only to insects," he said smiling.

And for the first time since the beginning of the whole ordeal, there was soft laughter among the group... In-The-Woods smiled as well. "Let us not underestimate our enemies, for even prairie birds have their ranks in nature."

"They have their ranks among my favorite foods as well," Left-Wing chimed in again. There was a low laughter within the lodge. "Blue-Leaf is a warrior. Let him earn his feathers."

In-The-Woods slowly nodded his head. "When the time comes, you will know which group you fall into. The Inner Council has much to discuss, decisions to make. Decisions that cannot be left to the rash of youth." The elder paused momentarily, and then asked, "Are there any questions concerning what has been divulged thus far?"

"What of the stranger? The one White-Sun calls the Deer-Lady?" Tall-Eagle asked. "She is far too ill to travel with the main group. Let her stay with us, for we will be here a few suns longer, giving her more time to rest."

In-The-Woods flipped the question over in his mind. But before he was able to speak... another voice spoke instead. A voice that was low and melodious. "I am White-Sun, and I speak not only for the women of our band, but for those under my care as well." She paused, as if awaiting someone to challenge her authority. Nobody spoke. "It would be unwise to take the stranger, the one I named the Deer-Lady. For she will slow you down greatly. And as her care-taker, I should stay behind as well."

The second elder, Bright-Arrow, scoffed at the notion. "We will be traveling with the young ones," he said to her. "What if one were to fall ill?"

"Then Mocking-Bird will care for them," another elder said.

"Mocking-Bird will be by my side. Where she belongs," White-Sun said. Bright-Arrow went to object... but her expression said more forcefully than any words ever could. They all lapsed into a deep silence.

"Tomorrow you will all know where you belong," In-The-Woods said slowly. "But tonight, let us celebrate with the rest."

The lodge slowly emptied itself out as each person made their way to the dance. Soon they were surrounded by dancers and laughter as the drummers drummed and the singers sang. And slowly... the tension and stress of their dire situation began to melt away.

After gaining as much information as he could, Red-River tapped Black-Feather on the shoulder. The two then started to slide backwards on their stomachs... slowly making their way through the grass. Their muscles were extremely tense and sore when they finally made it back to the tree line... for they had to crawl the entire way.

The half-moon stood high and proud in the sky... illuminating the prairie far and wide. Many times the two had to resist the impulse to move too quickly... they knew Lakota scouts were on point. But now... in the safety of the shadows of the trees... the two allowed themselves to relax fully.

"We now have a headcount," Red-River said to his companion. "Their numbers are far greater than ours right now."

"But soon that will change," Black-Feather said.

"Indeed it will. But as for now, as of right now, we do not yet possess sufficient support in this territory. All that we can do is track their every move. Not let them escape."

"Escape?" Black-Feather said derisively... somewhat wanting to laugh. "They celebrate."

Red-River shot him an icy glare... but did not respond verbally.

The wind carried the pounding of the drum across the prairie and through the trees. And if one were to listen slightly more... they could hear the songs and laughter as well. "You are to stay here," he instructed Black-Feather. "Before the rising of the sun, somebody will be here to relieve you."

Black-Feather said noting as he turned to face the direction of the Lakota.

In silence, Red-River turned and went to where his horse was tethered to a tree. He was eager to return to his own campsite where he could nurse his hatred for the Lakota for keeping what is rightfully his... and to strategize on ways of getting her back.

The shrilling scream of a war-cry jarred Red-River from his peaceful dreams. It felt as if he had just fallen asleep when the war-whoop jerked him suddenly into startled alertness. With sleep clouded eyes he looked up just as arrows were ripping into his tipi. The arrows fell harmlessly to the ground, for their effective energy had been spent on the impact.

He could hear the thrumming of horse hooves as more war-cries shattered the early morning air. Quickly he grabbed his own bow and arrows and emerged from his lodge completely naked.

The first light of the day seemed deep and vague in the morning mist. The world around them seemed gray and misty... with a dream-like quality to everything. Soon the sun would rise and the mist will be gone. But in the camp of the Crow... what will the light of the rising sun fall upon? Death and destruction?

More war-cries pierced the air as a mass of unknown warriors rolled through the camp... spurring their horses like angry hornets. Their cries pierced the Crow men with cold needles of horror and despair. They all emerged from their own tipis and then began scrambling for safety... often stumbling over their own fallen brothers of war.

The angry attackers filled the morning air with raining arrows as they fired in distinguishingly into the camp. From their feathers and clothing... Red-River knew they were the Lakota... the very people who were holding Bull's-Tail. Their high-cheek boned faces were brightly painted. Their impressive appearance seemed supremely confident and deadly.

Red-River found himself shaking all over. Rather it was from fear or anger or the chill of the air against his naked body... he did not know. But still, he gathered his strength and fitted an arrow into his bow. A few Lakota warriors had gathered atop of a distance hill... no doubt preparing for another wave of attacks. He aimed at the group and allowed the arrow to fly. It fell well short of its target.

"Get your weapons!" he cried out to the Crow in unmistakable anger. In the chaos... his rapid pulse made his ears ring. "Bring the horses!" he ordered. But their horses had already been scattered.

Upon cold and stiff legs... the Crow men tried to rush to their lodges for their tools of war... only to find their tipis were slowly smoldering with growing flames.

Here comes another wave... Red-River could hear the horse's hooves floating on the liquid air. Gathering his breath he shouted again... encouraging the Crow to kill the Lakota attackers. He, himself knelt immediately and withdrew another arrow. Pulling on the bowstring he felt the feather tickling his cheek as he ran his eyes along the arrow's shaft. The equestrians rode swiftly into range and Red-River released the deadly projectile. It sailed through the air with deadly speed and landed with a sickening slap in a horse's neck.

The horse came to a jolting halt as its rider was thrown from its back. Red-River took on a savage pride as he let out his own battle cry. But his celebration was premature.

The thrown rider slowly got to his feet and tried clearing his cloggy mind by shaking his head. Aside from the mud and blood that caked his face, Red-River knew the man would live.

In anger, he withdrew another arrow. But before he could fit it, another equestrian came striding through the camp towards the fallen Lakota. Red-River took aim at the second horseman... but the arrow had missed its target.

The second horseman had reached the fallen Lakota and held out a hand to him. In a single jump, the fallen Lakota leaped up behind him upon the horse's back. Riding swiftly the two rode outside the range of arrows.

The sun… still low in the morning sky etched a golden silhouette around the knoll of the eastern hills. Full flames were now crackling and spitting from their tipis… curling tongues of fire reaching up towards the heavens. He became bitterly angry as he watched his own lodge floating into the morning sky on wings of smoke and fire.

Around twenty Lakota warriors had regrouped upon another hill. They stayed atop their horses as they looked back over the Crow's camp. Even from that distance, they could tell their horses were exhausted… for when they breathed out… thick plumes of gray fog flared from their nostrils… and it was doing so in rapid successions.

In an attempt to calm his tautened nerves… Red-River let out another war-cry. Other Crow followed suit. Although he was still naked… he became warm by the spreading fires. Fires that were everywhere… shooting hungry flames forward…. looking for something else to devour.

Unexpectantly… the Lakota war party had split up. Red-River became confused. Despite the many waves of attack… there hasn't been a single fatality. There were many injuries… but a single life has yet to be lost. Before he could rationalize the situation… a wave of horsemen came riding towards their campsite… screaming and yelping as they furiously rode.

Red-River called out to his Crow… telling them to take careful aim. More arrows filled the air as both sides opened fire. Many missed their targets. A few found their mark. Agonizing cries of pain seemed to be swallowed up in the heat of the raging waves of fire. A couple of the horsemen took up their lances and war clubs… threading their horses expertly through the campsite… swinging their weapons with all their might… screaming and yelping with all their primal fury.

Rolling curtains of thick smoke covered the campsite… overshadowing the sun as it became a blood-red ball that hovered over the eastern hills. The second Lakota war party appeared in the North of the camp. The swarming reinforcement party road fast and hard through the tattered and ruined campsite.

Again Red-River survived a deadly barrage of arrows that rained from the heavens... but the agonizing cries of the slowly dying we're everywhere. And again the Lakota attackers gathered upon the hill... where they sat overlooking the Crow campsite. Occasionally a lone warrior would draw near... firing a random shot at the Crow as they went about tending the wounded and trying to extinguish many fires.

Red-River had to dress and whatever clothes he could scavenge... for his lodge and all it contained was devoured by fire. The buckskin outfit hung somewhat loosely from his body... the leggings were shiny and slick with wear. The Crow men worked feverishly to save what they could... but very little remain. There was only destruction and the injured victims of the Lakota aggression.

Most of the campsite laid blackened... smoldering with thick, black smoke that hung in the morning sky... creating a gray curtain that shrouded the morning sun. A semblance of a breeze had come up from the West... causing the smoke to drift lazily towards the sun... again turning it blood red. Red-River instantly recalled seeing those same skies reflecting the same destructive fires in a war against the Pikuni... a band of the Blackfoot Confederacy. There, the Crow used fires to destroy their enemies... enemies that were enveloped in angry flames... enemies that died horribly... shrieking in agony.

Red-River became grimly delighted at the thought of his new enemies dying in the same horrible fashion. But his fantasy came to an abrupt end as the burning pain of an arrow pierced his side.

Though pain clouded eyes Red-River look down to his side. Pain flowed freely as warm blood wept from an arrow that protruded from his flesh. He gripped the shaft of the arrow with both hands... trying to keep it from moving.

Slowly, he looked up... only to find a loan Lakota warrior staring at him... his eyes ablaze with triumph. The Lakota warrior was on foot.

Filled with raw anger... Red-River gripped the shaft, then broke the arrow's wooden body as close as he could to its entry wound. The Lakota warrior looked upon Red-River with a kind of renewed wonder... but instantly his eyes harden as they challenge the Crow from across the clearing of smoldering fires.

Red-River watched as his hand reached back to draw an arrow. He watched as the Lakota's arrow rise until it was aimed steadily at his chest... then rise a little higher until it was trained at his face.

Looking past the flint tip... looking beyond the hand and arrow shaft... Red-River found himself looking into the eyes of someone very young. Again he felt the instant sting of anger and hatred scalding his heart... for he knew this warrior was trying to prove his bravery... trying to use the life of Red-River to bolster his own reputation.

Red-River let out a fierce battle cry that seems to drown out all other sounds. He watched as the Lakota's fingers release the arrow... the arrow seemed to disappear into a swift-moving blur. A blur that pierced his cheek. But the pain of the flesh wound never followed.

In quick strides, Red-River cross the clearing... rushing the young Lakota warrior before he could withdraw another arrow. Startled by the sudden attack... the young warrior's hand trembled as it reached for another arrow.

A costly mistake.

The powerful blow of Red-River was fierce and sudden... and the Lakota's nose gave way under the heavy hand of the Crow. The Lakota yelped in pain as a spray of blood filled the air.

Red-River knew instantly that he had broken the nose of the Lakota... for he could feel the cartilage crumble on impact. The Lakota stumbled backward... trying to keep from falling into the dark haze of unconsciousness... a steady stream of blood flowing from his nose.

The Lakota dropped his bow and tried clawing desperately for another tool of war... his tomahawk ... but the attack of Red-River was relentless and in an instinct, he saw an explosion of stars behind closed eyelids as he received another vicious blow to his face. The Lakota couldn't keep from falling.

Red-River could feel the onslaught of anxious adrenaline as he watched the young one fall to the ground. In a swift motion he was upon the fallen warrior... straddling him between his legs... and there... driven by anger he began to punch into the soft wetness of the man's face.

Red-River was so engrossed in the easy victory that he didn't see or hear the yelping Lakota horsemen as they formed a swarming reinforcement party. All he felt was the sudden burst of pain as a lance struck him across his gape… quickly followed by a cold darkness that seemed to embrace his soul… luring him into the realms of unconsciousness.

At that very moment… In-The-Woods and Bright-Arrow were leading the Little-Star people over the tall grasses… across the rolling lands… towards the very edge of the Great Plains.

Left-Wing drop from the horse he road and knelt beside his fallen cousin, Blue-Leaf. The accompanying Lakota formed a moving circle around the two with their horses… creating a protective barrier between them and the angry Crow.

Blue-Leaf's head swam in a swirling haze of confusion. With blurry and watery eyes he looked up at his cousin… only to find Left-Wing smiling mischievously down upon him.

"You went to count coup but ended up being counted," Left-Wing said over the heavy hooves of the circling horses. He then turned his attention to the following Crow… the Crow now laid face down in the wet grass of the early morning. "He is there if you still want to count. But it counts only for half, for I believe I have sent him to the realm of the spirits already," he says smiling as he gestured with his chin.

Blue-Leaf said nothing. Instead, he probed with soft fingers around his nose… wincing at the sharp pain. "It is broken, cousin," he said to Left-Wing.

"As is your pride," Left-Wing said laughing. "Let us go now, for the Crow seem to be gathering for a counterattack."

Slowly, Blue-Leaf rose to his feet. All around him were his people... protecting him as they set atop their horses... tails and manes flowing and tossing in the wind of their speed.

Left-Wing retrieved his horse... and in a liquid motion was a top of the magnificent creature. Blue-Leaf leapt up behind him... finding comfort and safety upon the horse... for he knew the horse was swift... therefore providing a quick escape if needed.

Once on the horses back... Blue-Leaf had a new vantage view of the battlefield. And there he saw the carnage and destruction left in the wake of the lethal encounter. He saw flames as they embraced the charred ruins of a tipi... quickly catching the soft leather on fire. Many Crow laid upon the ground... withering in pain and agony as the earth drank their blood.

Despite the injury sustained in the battle... Blue-Leaf felt the gathering pride swelling in his heart as he looked upon the savagery and cruelty against those that had broken his nose.

He then felt the horse lurch into motion... riding swiftly through the campsite and up the hill... needing no urging or guidance from Left-Wing. And there they stayed... watching as the battered Crow tried piecing together what was left of their tattered camp.

A searing pain... like scolding lava ran the full length of Red-River's body. Still, his head throbbed with every heartbeat as his mind slowly made his way back to the realm of the living... to the realm of consciousness.

The light of the sun had drained from the sky... leaving the rolling hills a monochromatic gray and black... the two hues effortlessly blending into one another. Red-River knew the moon would soon appear... bathing the dark world with its icy warm glow. And in this glow, he will be able to fully examine the extent of his injury. But until then… he could only explore his injury blindly with trembling hands. He felt the arrow wound had been bandaged.

"Have you returned?" a voice whispered from the darkness. "Or do you still rests between worlds?"

"I am here," Red-River rasped with a pasty tongue.

There was a soft rustling as the unknown Crow reached out to comfort Red-River. "I have feared you would cross over fully, for you received a mighty powerful blow," he whispered.

Blinking against the pain that enveloped his head… he tried recalling what had occurred. But only fractured images flashed before his mind's eye. Images that could not be deciphered. "Who are you? And why do you whisper?"

"It's is I, Bare-Foot. I whisper because the Lakota's are near." He then ran his fingers over Red-River's bandages… fingertips probing in his handiwork in expert fashion. "Your side injury wasn't as bad as it looked. The arrow has been removed."

Red-River knew the Crow warrior Bare-Foot. His father was a Medicine-Man before he was lost in the war against the Cheyenne. But his father had taught Bare-Foot many a thing as a child… things that had aided the tribe in the bloody aftermath of war. "The Lakota are still here? How long have I been in between worlds?"

"We were attacked this morning. Everything has been lost. This is why you lay upon the grass instead of sheltered within a lodge. All day the Sioux sat upon the hill. And all day we feared another attack. But the attack never came. Instead, they sat upon their horses and watched us. Just before the falling of the sun, many of the Sioux road out. But a few stayed upon that hill. Waiting. Watching. We fear they have drawn near in the dark of night. But only the light of the moon would tell."

Red-River remembered that hill… and how they arrogantly set upon their steeds. Their black hair was braided in red leather… which sat upon their shoulders. Their heads were crowned with an impressive array of feathers. Feathers that seemed to glow in the rays of the early morning sun. Their war paint bold and colorful. "Such arrogance," he said finally… his voice returning to its usual rasping hardness.

"They scattered our horses. In the dark of night we sent scouts out to find and return them. We don't even know if they slipped undetected past the Lakota," Bare-Foot said.

Red-River turned his gaze towards the hill the Lakota had conquered... but the shadows enshrouded the grassy knoll. "How many Crow lives have been lost?" he finally asked.

"Four. And many have been injured. Too many to launch an effective counter-attack. But soon our allies will arrive. Then we will wipe them from this earth. And their memory will die with us."

In his words... Red-River found comfort. "They stayed. They celebrated. And soon they will perish," he said sadistically. And then a sinister grin danced upon his thin lips. "And then I will have what is rightfully mine."

Bare-Foot knew he was speaking about the strange woman... the woman who had murdered Red-River's brother. And because of this murder, Bare-Foot presumed he was speaking of vengeance... something that is rightfully his according to Crow law. "It is a shame she must die. For she is a beautiful woman, in her own strange way."

Red-River said nothing... but could still feel the burning asset of jealousy smoldering within as barefoot spoke upon Bull-Tail's. And it was then did he realize the true depths of his predicament... and how treacherous the path he has chosen truly is. He intended to retrieve Bull's-Tail... and the only way this could be achieved is with the aid of the Crow and their allies. But with the assistance of his people... according to their loss... the woman must be put to death. But Red-River could not allow this. He would not allow this. The only solution is to retrieve the woman and then disappear with her in the rising sun... leaving behind everything he had ever known. And the more he thought about Bull-Tails... the more assured he became that he would Indy sacrifice all for.

With the dawn breaking for off to the east... a soft golden glow in a vague and dirty gray sky brought a sign of a good day. At least it did to Tall-Eagle.

As custom dictated... he greeted the coming of a new day with a silent prayer of thanks... offering tobacco to the seven sacred directions. After doing so he returned to his usual routine. Before long the site of The-Little-Star band was swarming with activities.

In the absence... the warriors were doing the work of the women... retrieving buffalo hides from the muddy riverbanks so that they may be de-fleshed. Others went about preparing buffalo meat so that they may be cured by the smoke and slow heat of smudged fires. A few of the young warriors were preparing to deer... hanging the creature by its hooves upon smoke poles. Then with a flint knife... inserting it in an expert fashion so that its belly opened and spilled its inners onto the ground.

The men knew that most of these things will be set ablaze once they broke camp... for they would need to travel light and fast if they wished to rejoin In-The-Woods and his band. But even with his knowledge... they still took pride in the work... knowing all the work was for naught.

Just after midday... Pretty-Elk pointed out tall shafts of signal smoke towards the direction of the Crow's camp. Even from the vast distance... Tall-Eagle could easily see the black smoke lazily drifting towards the heavens.

"Is that not foolish? To send such visible signs while trapped in Sioux territory?" Pretty-Elk asked Tall-Eagle. "Does this not pinpoint their location?"

"Perhaps this is a sign of ill omen?" Tall-Eagle said. "For what if the Crow knows her allies are near? Would this not be an easy way of telling them exactly where they are?"

"This is true, this is true," Pretty-Elk said as he continued to look upon the smoke signals. "Yesterday morning we surprised the Crow with an attack. Last night, I could not find sleep, for in my heart I feared today they will return the surprise."

Tall-Eagle respectfully said nothing. Pretty-Elk was no doubt a warrior. But there was also no room for doubt that he preferred peace.

Tall-Eagle and others suspected him to be two spirited... but never openly discussed it with anybody. If this was true... then perhaps it will be revealed once one of the two spirits dies... leaving either anger and hostility or self-loathing and self-pity in its place.

"Leave no room for doubt, they will come," Tall-Eagle assured Pretty-Elk. "Yesterday, as I stood watch over the Crow camp, I saw how they went about tending their dead and wounded, scavenging what they could. I watched as the Crow went about their scavenging like it was a fever ant hill. I have witnessed their resilience... the resourcefulness. And I was impressed."

"' Impressed?' By the simplistic and primitive Crow?" Pretty-Elk asked.

"Indeed. Do not underestimate the Crow, my friend. When a wolf has gone mad, it will not feel the tip of your arrow nor the thrust of your spear. It will continue to attack because that's all it knows. The ruthless and primitive Crow is like a wolf that has gone mad, it doesn't know its limitation nor the fact that it is injured."

"You speak too highly of these Crow," Left-Wing said as he drew near. "I still think we should have ended their story in our attacks yesterday."

"We cannot sacrifice our warriors to hatred, my friend," Tall-Eagle said evenly. "We had the element of surprise working in our favor when we first attacked. But they quickly recovered and we were running low on arrows."

"Is that not why we have spears and tomahawks?" Left-Wing asked antagonistically.

"For close-range war? Yes. But in order for these things to be effective, we would have to be in range of their arrows."

Pretty-Elk slowly nodded his head in agreement... but Left-Wing said nothing more.

"You just came back from watching the Crow's campsite, did you not?" Tall-Eagle asked Left-Wing.

"I did," he responded. "Still they lick their wounds."

"What of the smoke signals?"

"Of that, I am not sure," Left-Wing responded as he gazed off into the distance... watching as the black smoke drifted toward the home of the Great-Mystery. "Perhaps they are signaling their allies?"

"We had thought the same," Pretty-Elk chimed in.

"Have you checked on my cousin, Blue-Leaf?" Left-Wing asked as he turned back towards Tall-Eagle. The acting chief slowly shook his head. "How about the Deer-Lady?" he asked as he flashed a tight mischievous grin.

"You speak as if this would be wrong," Tall-Eagle said.

"Is she not under your care?" Left-Wing asked... but Tall-Eagle sensed something in the undercurrent of his tone. Instantly, Left-Wing could feel annoyance radiating from Tall-Eagle. "And how is she?" he asked his acting chief... wanting to defuse the tension... at least temporarily.

"I have yet to see her," he said truthfully. "But still she rests." He then lapsed into a cold silence. All day the acting chief fought the unyielding urge to visit the Deer-Lady. He wanted so desperately to visit her... to watch her sleep once again... but knew he could not admit this to anyone... let alone Left-Wing. "Soon I would check in on the Deer-Lady. And your cousin if this is your wish."

"My wish is to do away with the Crow," Left-Wing said in a somewhat anxious tone. "But Blue-Leaf has suffered a shattered ego. An injury that is very difficult to overcome," he said as he lowered his voice and mock sadness. This invoked a small chuckle from both Tall-Eagle and Pretty-Elk.

"Tall-Eagle! Somebody approaches!" No-Horn yelled frantically as he brought his horse to an abrupt stop. He then leapt to the ground and quickly approach to three warriors. "An old man approaches from the south," he said as he stopped before the acting chief.

"Does he pose a threat?"

"I do not know. I do not recognize his clothing, for they are not made of buckskin. Nor is he wearing feathers."

Tall-Eagle stood in silence... thinking over the information he was provided.

"The scouts are tracking him. They have not alerted the old one to their presents. They are waiting for me to return with instructions,"

No-Horns said... trying to gently persuade the acting Chief to respond quickly.

"Return with him," Tall-Eagle said to Left-Wing. "If you sense danger, may your arrows fly true."

"And if I do not?" he asked Tall-Eagle.

"Then let him approach. Perhaps he could provide us with information. Or trade."

At once both No-Horns and Left-Wing were gone. Left-Wing to retrieve his own horse, and No-Horn to lead the way.

"If he is an elder and comes in peace, we must treat him as such," Tall-Eagle said to Pretty-Elk.

"Indeed," he said simply then turn to retrieve what was needed to honor a weary traveler.

Slowly, Tall-Eagle begins to make his way towards the center of the camp... the place where the honor ceremony will take place if the old one comes in peace. And once again he found himself thinking about the Deer-Lady... and once again he felt his heart as it swelled and filled with this new kind of comforter that warmed it. A kind of comfort that left when Girl-Lost crossed over to the Land-Of-The-Spirits. A warmth his aching heart longed for... and soon he felt himself smiling.

But his mouth quickly fading when he glanced towards the heavens at the rising smoke signals... and again was plunged back into the dark reality of their plight... and the unavoidable bloodshed this flight would reap. Blood of his people... especially if the acting Chief made the wrong call and as always... since his elective obligation was assigned to him... he felt himself being torn between hope and resignation.

"Somebody approaches!" a yell came from just beyond the camp. Tall-Eagle instantly knew the traveler posed no threat... for if he did... Left-Wing would have never allowed him to pass their line of hidden scouts.

Tall-Eagle went to the edge of the camp and saw the lone rider and his weary pony struggle up the final hill. The acting chief saw that the stranger's clothing was indeed odd. They seemed very light... and very soft to the touch. Tall-Eagle had seen such clothing worn by the People-of-the-Great-Sands on one of his many journeys. A place where its villages were carved in the faces of rock towers... and he had seen their attire. It was something closely akin to their clothing. Only not as heavy. And upon the Old-One's head sat something strange. And strapped to it was something that seemed to shimmer and shine... reflecting the sun's light more clearer than any calm lake.

The stranger's clothing he wore upon his crown had cast a shadow over his eyes. His dark brown walnut-face was deeply grooved with wrinkles... and his long white hair fell from under the garment he wore on his head... and fell over his slumped shoulders.

Tall-Eagle told Standing-Bull and New-Calf, two-horse watchers, to assist the Old-One into the camp.

"Do you come in peace?" Tall-Eagle asked as New-Calf tried to help the old one to the ground.

"Peace?" the Old-One asked as he snorted in exclamation. "My young friend, I fear I come to you in pieces," he chuckled as he brushed aside the helping hand of New-Calf. The Old-One spoke with an unexpected steady note of youth and vitality. And once he crawled down from the tired pony... he stood proud and erect. And the way he held his head up high gave him more the air of a warrior than an old man. But the man was no doubt well beyond his fighting years.

"I do not understand," Tall-Eagle said.

"I may not look scared, but I have the body of a warrior that has live many lives over. And the wounded soul of a man who has seen it all. Therefore, I come to you in pieces." There seem to be an undercurrent of a smile in his sad words... a type of cryptic truth that comes only with the wisdom of the ages.

"I am Tall-Eagle, acting chief of The-Little-Star band," he said as he slightly bowed his head. "We are a clan, a branch of the Lakota."

"The Lakota?" The old man asked as he slowly nodded his head. "A part of the mighty Sioux Nation, who no doubtedly just emerged from your winter's cocoon only to pursue the dusty buffalo herds."

"Indeed, we have," Tall-Eagle responded. "What is your name, old one?"

The old man stood silently for a few moments... staring intensely towards the pony's hoofs. At last, the old man looked up... and

Tall-Eagle could see a deep sadness lurking within the depths of his shaded eyes. Deeply sad... but not unhappy. "I have so many, I know not which one to give," came a cryptic whisper finally.

At that very moment, Pretty-Elk and White-Sun approached, carrying bags of water. Pretty-Elk handed Standing-Bull a bag while White-Sun gave hers to the traveler. The old man gratefully accepted the water... licking his dry lips with the tip of his tongue. He then sipped the water with slow deliberation... savoring it with a dry tongue and throat.

Standing-Bull stroked the pony's neck with his free hand... then held the water so that the pony could have his share. As it drank noisily, Tall-Eagle ran his eyes the full length of the traveler... then stopped at the shiny frame that was strapped to the strange thing that sat upon his head. He wanted to reach out and touch it... but did not.

"It is a buckle. Given to me by the people with pale faces," the traveler said in between sips.

Tall-Eagle looked down into the man's eyes... and found the traveler staring at him intensely.

"I got the hat from them as well. Would you like to see it?" he asked as he removed the black hat and handed it to Tall-Eagle. The acting chief turn the garment over in his hands... studying it with keen eyes.

"The buckle is made of pure silver," the traveler said as he watched Tall-Eagle staring at his own reflection. "Taken from a land they call the dark continent."

Slowly Tall-Eagle handed the traveler back the hat, then looked at the approaching Mocking-Bird. In her arms she carried the clan's Medicine Bundle. And within this bundle laid the band sacred Ceremonial Pipe.

The traveler had encountered the Sioux many times... so he was familiar with the customs of the People-of-the-Plains.

The two sat upon a blanket in the center of the camp. The traveler sat facing east... the way of the Morning-Star. This made Tall-Eagle believe that perhaps he was Cheyenne.

Once the prayers were offered and the pipe was filled... the traveler took a long, deep draw from the pipe stem and then held in the smoke. With eyes closed, he began to pray. As he spoke silently... smoke rolled from his lips. And then he touched the stem of the pipe to his forehead and handed it to Tall-Eagle.

Tall-Eagle watched as the traveler blew the remaining smoke into cupped hands... then ran his ancient hands over the top of his greyish-white hair. The acting chief followed suit... sending his own prayers to the One-Who-Had-Created all.

Slowly, the sun made its way across the heavens on its celestial journey. The clouds billowing high in the outer realms... playing and dancing with each other. Throughout the day Tall-Eagle had conversed deeply with a traveler... speaking upon a number of subjects.

Tall-Eagle knew the man was well-traveled... journeying well beyond the limits of Turtle-Island. And he listened intently as he described the many lands... the many peoples... the many cultures. As they strolled slowly through the camp... physically he continued to walk beside the old man... but with the vivid descriptions and guided imagery... mentally and spiritually he was in a land far beyond the rising of the sun.

Although they had walked and talked throughout the day... Tall-Eagle knew not the traveler's name... nor the name of his tribe.

"I have been called many things, my young friend," he had told Tall-Eagle earlier that day.

"Since I have not been given a name, and since your clothing and jewelry are strange, and since your mannerisms are strange, I shall call you the Strange-One," Tall-Eagle announced.

Upon hearing the name, the traveler chuckled bitterly. "Of all the names you could have chosen, you have chosen the one I am most commonly known as." He then fell into a deep silence.

"White-Sun is preparing food for the two of you," Mocking-Bird said as she approached the talking men. "Soon it will be finished, and she will take it to the center of the camp." With this being said she turned abruptly and return in the direction of what she came.

As the two slowly made their way back towards the center of the camp, Tall-Eagle asked, "You say your hat and clothing come from those with pale faces. Tell me Strange-One, what are they truly like?"

At the question, an ominous-like shadow clouded the travelers face. He walked in silence... looking left nor right. Only straight towards the ground. But even from his profile... Tall-Eagle could see the sadness lurking within the depths of his eye.

Before long the two sat upon a soft blanket... patiently awaiting the cooking of White-Sun. The traveler had yet to say anything. Finally, he spoke. "I have lived long. Long enough to see the fall of mighty nations. And I can only say this of the people to the South and the East, all the great chiefs are dead, only the worms that fed upon decaying flesh is what remains of these great Nations." And then he fell silent once again.

Tall-Eagle sat in stunned silence... tossing the torrid remarks over in his mind. For great chiefs... he considered the statement as the most unkind and unwarranted description.

"My heart speaks clearly at last," the travelers said as if reading the thoughts of Tall-Eagle. "The pale-faces. Mouths that devour with tongues that speak of lies and deception. Of self-entitlement and vanity. With eyes that are blinded or filled with lust. And elders with hearts that have grown cold to the natural world. For they are enemies of the Natural World. They are enemies of men, for they set man against man in order to control the natural world."

Tall-Eagle said nothing. Instead, he repeatedly jabbed a stick at the fire that burned low before them. But what could he say? What kind of experience did he have with that primitive side of life? To be an enemy to Mother-Earth? He could barely grasp what was being said.

"I could sense much tension in the camp," the traveler had finally said.

"Indeed, there is." Tall-Eagle began to explain how they are now at war with the Crow. How they had come across the strange woman with a long and narrow face... how they rescued her from the malicious Crow and their wrath for vengeance. He told the traveler about the attack at the Crows camp the morning before, and how they are waiting for a counter-attack. He said nothing of In-The-Woods and the party that travels with him.

"Is this why you continue to watch the smoke signals?" he asked Tall-Eagle.

"We believe they may be signaling the ones who will join them in battle against us. But of this we are not for sure," the acting chief responded. "Tell me, Strange-One, how is it that you speak Lakota so well?"

"I went to live amongst the Turtle-Bear-Clan. But this was many winters ago."

"How many languages do you speak?"

"Many. I speak many languages. And I understand even more."

"I know many as well. Of course not as many as a man who is as well traveled as you. But the one we call the Deer-Lady, she spoke a language that was completely alien to me. It was a tone and dialect I have never encountered before. And I have encountered many."

The Traveler didn't respond to the statement.

"Her look is strange as well," Tall-Eagle continued. "Unlike any woman I've encountered, she is very thin. And she seems quite tall. Have you ever encountered a place where the women are tall and thin?"

"There are places," the Strange-One replied simply.

"Every man, woman, and child I've encountered were powerfully-built. Ready to do the intense labor that life requires of them. And her face is very narrow. Narrow to the point where her mouth protrudes from her face. Like a deer," he said as he thought of the unkind description given by White-Sun. "But very beautiful," he quickly added.

Again the two grew silent. And Tall-Eagle went back to probing at the fire. For a brief moment, the situation reminded the acting chief of his younger days... when he was an anxious child eager for stories at the side of his grandfather... jabbing impatiently at the fire before then.

The thought brought a genuine smile to his hardened face.

"The one you call the Deer-Lady still rest?"

"She does," Tall-Eagle said as he was jerked back from the peaceful days of yesteryear. "Do you think you could tell us where she is from if you were to see her?" he asked hopefully.

"Perhaps, I could narrow it down a bit. But to tell you of her true origins may be quite difficult."

Tall-Eagle and the Strange-One entered the lodge of White-Sun. There they found the woman bathed in shadows. Although the sun was sinking outside the tipi... it still took a moment for the eyes to adjust to the shadows.

White-Sun was dipping her fingers into a bowl of water... then putting her wet fingers to the lips of the Deer-Lady... allowing small droplets of water to fall from her finger-tips into the woman's mouth. Tall-Eagle and the Strange-One watched when suddenly the stranger gasped for air.

Tall-Eagle turned to the old man, whose face seen frozen with stunned recognition. The Strange-Ones took a hesitant step forward... his eye staring intensely at the Deer-Lady. Slowly his eyes went to her wild, curly hair... then methodically work their way down the full length of her thin frame. Then he said something in a strange language... the language he heard spoken by the Deer-Lady.

"Do you know her?" Tall-Eagle asked. But the Strange-Ones didn't respond... instead, he took another step towards that Deer-Lady... absorbed the beauty and elegance of the sleeping woman. White-Sun shot the old man a look of confusion. "Do you know her?" Tall-Eagle asked again... his words a little more forceful.

With great effort, the Strange-One pulled his gaze away from the sleeping woman and turn them toward Tall-Eagle. His eyes were filled with excitement.

"Do you know her, Strange-One?" Tall-Eagle repeated. Within the depths of the old man's eyes, he saw something flicker. The old man seemed to hesitate for a brief moment... as if to deal with some unspoken emotion that swayed in his heart.

Finally, truth won out... and the old man decided that truth is what this warrior shall here. Even if the truth were to confuse him. "This woman is a direct descendant of the Gods," he said somberly as he returned his gaze to the sleeping woman.

"What?" Tall-Eagle asked confusingly. "'The gods'? There is but one Creator, Strange-One. A man as well traveled as you should know these things."

"This is true, my young friend. There is but one Creator. But there have been many gods and goddesses throughout the world. Ancient gods and goddesses who mated with mankind... spreading their superior seed throughout all the world's nations," the old man gently corrected. "This woman, Tall-Eagle, she is a descendant of these gods and goddesses."

Tall-Eagle first looked at the old man... then looked down upon the Deer-Lady... studying her strange hair... her protruding face... her fragile and thin build. Tall-Eagle could see beyond her current disheveled appearance... wild and rugged... yet deeply beautiful. From her, he felt a kind of profound kinship due to her vulnerability. But not the raw power of reverence due to the presence of a goddess.

Tall-Eagle chuckled to himself as he turned to leave the lodge... chuckling at the old man's foolishness. "Let us leave these two in peace, Strange-One," Tall-Eagle said as he led the way out.

"I know you mock me, young warrior. But my words are true," he said without taking his eyes off the sleeping woman. "I've seen her image before. Carved on solid rock in the ancient cities."

The reference to the ancient cities instantly drew Tall-Eagle's attention. He recalled the many legends and stories his mother told him as a child. The stories of ancient cities made of solid rock... created by an ancient civilization who had mapped the vastness of the heavens. But these were no more than childhood stories. Stories to entertain a weak and feeble mind.

Tall-Eagle looked towards a sleeping woman. Although the light of the world continued to dim... even in the shadows he could see the long sweep of her graceful neck. This woman is indeed strangely beautiful. But surely she is no descendant of God's, he reasoned with himself. "Come, Strange-One. I want to hear more of these ancient cities." He then lifted the flap of the tipi... and the sun's last light entered. For a brief moment, the two men stared at the play of pale lights that splashed across her face.

Stepping out into the coolness of the spring evening... the two men made their way back to the center... where the small fire burned. Again they took their seats. Tall-Eagle stared at the old man... waiting patiently for him to speak. But the Strange-One simply stared into the small fire.

"When I was a child," Tall-Eagle began, "My mother would regale me with great tales of an ancient city, a city by the way of the south wind. She told me these stories were told to her by her mother... and told by her mother before that. So told me of cities that touch the heavens. But as I grew, I reasoned the stories grew into legends with the telling and retelling... growing into myths with the passage of time. But I don't think there is any truth to them."

"The stories of the ancient cities are true," the Strange-One said without taking his eyes from the fire. "I have been there. I have seen the ruins of this great civilization with my own eyes." The man then lapsed into a hard silence.

Tall-Eagle turned in his seat... staring into the ancient eyes of the Strange-One. "The language you spoke to her. It was her language. Is that the language of these Gods?"

The Strange-One chuckled somberly to himself. "Yes and no," he said finally... his voice became thick with emotion. "No, because it is the language of man. The man who conquered and destroyed the cities. Yes because only God could invoke such wanton death and destruction in their wake. For I have seen these gods in war. I've watched as they used spears of fire and shiny metals to lay waste to entire civilizations... killing and murdering for the love of a yellow rock that they worship. Killing and murdering with evil atrocity as they claim their bloody prizes."

The old man had never turned his gaze from the fire. As he grew silent... his face was watchful and silent. It seemed to Tall-Eagle that the Strange-One was staring well beyond the small fire. Watching something else very far away. As if watching something in another realm.

"I have traveled long and far, my young friend. I have witnessed many, many things. But never had I witnessed such atrocities. When I was young... the last of the mighty cities were falling. The inhabitants died a slow and painful death. With the shiny metals, their flesh was stripped from their bones and fed to wild dogs. The man had their genitals removed and stuff in their mouth. The women had babies torn from their wombs… and the children were placed into bondage where they faced an unknown..." he let the sentence trail off. "Everywhere I turned stretched the ruins of war. The stench and decay of flesh. These gods would often conquer by way of fire. Sometimes I can still smell the stench of flesh as it sizzled and burned. When I fall into the realm of dreams, I can see these gods coming for me. Their pale faces peering and reaching out of the darkness that surrounds them."

Tall-Eagle had an eerie sensation the traveler was no longer speaking to him. Perhaps not even to himself. But instead to those who haunt his dreams. Tall-Eagle saw tears glittering in the light of the fire on the traveler's creviced cheeks. He let it fall freely... unnoticed. Or perhaps he did notice but didn't care. For an old warrior to shed a tear in the presence of another warrior was completely unheard of within the many warrior societies. But Tall-Eagle remained respectfully silent... for to acknowledge the vulnerability of falling tears with sympathetic words would not be in keeping with the warrior's society mentality. But he knew that traveler was aware that the young warrior was right beside him in his grief as he reminisced.

"The pale-face of the South, these gods, are they the same pale faces of those to the east? The Invaders?" Tall-Eagle finally asked

"No, Tall-Eagle," he said. "They are from another land. They too bring death and destruction, for many of them hold the same predatory inclination to obtain the yellow rocks that make them crazy. But their methods aren't as violent and brutal as the ones of old. But still, you will have to fight, or you will lose who you are. Your language, your culture, your name."

How can a man lose his name? Tall-Eagle asked himself as the old man's words reverberated in his head. *Nothing holds more power or glory than a name... for without a name... how can the spirits know who you are?*

Again the two sat in silence as Tall-Eagle sat thinking of all that he was told... he glanced over at the Strange-One. His dark eyes reflecting the suffering and torrid memories that tore at his heart. But still, he couldn't help but wonder how the old man associated the Deer-Lady with ancient gods. "You say you've seen her image carved into the Rocks. What did you mean?"

"The ancient cities were created in days so long ago that the time cannot be measured in winter counts. Her people, and the people before her people used signs and symbols that tell a story. And with these symbols... these stories have stood eternal and pure since they were first spoken. And will never change... but stand ever triumphal as they survive the rigors ravages of time. For the symbols have been carved into rocks... rocks that will last until the end of time. And I have seen pictures... faces of ancient gods and goddesses that came from the heavens to walk with mankind. I have sat for countless hours staring at these faces. This Deer-Lady, instantly I saw in her facial features aspects associated with the people called the Mayans. And the more I looked, I came to realize that she was the descendants of the gods... or some reincarnation of an ancient Queen."

The Strange-One knew talks of reincarnation was a strange subject to the Peoples of the Plains. He awaited Tall-Eagles questions concerning the topic. But instead, the young warrior questioned the religious beliefs of the stranger.

"You said these gods came to mate with the daughter's man? Why have the Lakota not heard of these Gods?" Tall-Eagle asked.

"Not all gods came to mate," the Strange-One said... gently correcting Tall-Eagle. "These gods and goddesses were teachers of men. They came to lead, to teach. But some were led astray by the beauty of women. And the Lakota do know of them. These gods are known by many names. The Invaders of the East call them angels or messiahs. In other lands they are known as lords. As light-bearers."

"And what are they known as to the Lakota?" Tall-Eagle asked... wanting to challenge the stranger's line of thinking.

"These gods are to them is what the White-Buffalo-Calf-Woman and the Wolf-Maiden is to the Lakota. But as I said... some were led astray and they mated it with humans. The Invaders of the East have what they call a 'Good book.' And in this book, it says that the sons of God came to Earth to mate with the daughters of man. The one you called the Deer-Lady, she is a descendant of one of these unions from another land. They are known as demigods."

The old man fell into a deep silence... as if given his words time to take root in the young warrior's mind.

He then continued, "I thought these demigods were nothing more than memories of ancient days. A time when the gods walked with men. And now it seems as if you have an angel in your presence. If indeed angels were ever more than legends of the conqueror's religion."

To the east... the sun had already sank behind the rim of the world. A soft and gentle wind swept through the hills of the grassy plains. Deep within the fading lights of the heavens were stars straining to be seen. Tall-Eagle knew that soon the vastness of the endless skies will be filled with stars. Stars shining brightly until the young moon takes her place... gently overpowering the light with her very own soft glow.

His mind turned back to the Deer-Lady... wondering if what the Strange-Ones said is true. His thoughts then turn towards the Invaders and his People's pending doom. For many winters there had been rumors of war floating on the winds. He, himself, had heard these terrible legends talked about in warrior circles. Stories of how the Invaders had laid waste to whole villages all along the Big-Water's edge. Setting flames to their dwellings and villages. Completely wiping out entire peoples. But of course such stories were widely exaggerated. Stories, again, told to entertain and frighten children. For how can a people become all but extinct? Driven from their homelands for the love of a yellow rock? Tall-Eagle couldn't fathom the thought.

The young warrior picked up a small twig and poked at the fire... "So you have seen these strange structures. What were they like?"

For the first time a genuine smile a dance upon the traveler's lips. "I have walked upon the floors of polished stone. Walked up the step pyramids and ran my fingers across the strange signs and symbols that were carved in the stones. And I assure you, my young friend. I have seen her image carved in these rocks... carved in the image of these ancient gods and goddesses."

Tall-Eagle sat in silence... just as he turned his attention back towards the old man, he heard the soft hoot of an imitation owl. The young warrior knew that such a sound constituted the gravest of threats.

"There's trouble, Strange-One," Tall-Eagle said to the old man. "I must go. But you are safe here." Tall-Eagle then dashed to his lodge where he gathered his weapons of war. Again he heard the soft hoot floating on a breeze. This sound was an alarm. But despite the unknown dangers... his warriors would never scream a warning overtly... for doing so would not only alert the enemy... but would spread panic through the campsite to no useful end.

The warrior quickened his steps.

Just outside the circle of tipis, he slowed his run. After looking into the light of the fire... he had to allow his eyes to fully adjust to the darkness. Again, he heard a soft hoot. At once he recognized the hoot belonging to Blue-Stalk. A second hoot, belonging to No-Horns sounded off towards the other side of the campsite.

With silent steps, he quickly made his way towards Blue-Stalk. He found his warrior friend wreathed in shadows... Tall-Eagle could barely make out his supine shape in the darkness. He dropped into the tall grass next to Blue-Stalk... taking advantage of the Plains natural cover.

"Crow," Blue-Stalk whispered.

Tall-Eagle's well-trained eyes traced the contours of the grassy hills. But they too were bathed in shadows.

"Listen to the silence," Blue-Stalk whispered as his eyes surveyed the scene. Tall-Eagle became suddenly aware that everything was indeed very quiet... as if the entire Plains laid in listening silence. "I distrust the silence," Blue-Stalk said, and then continued, "And the moon... it is early so she is but young and pale. But soon it will give enough light so that we may see our enemies." After saying this, Blue-Stalk let out another soft hoot.

"I believe they are awaiting the light of the moon as well," Tall-Eagle stated... his eyes still searching the hills for an enemy he still couldn't see. From behind they heard the soft rustling of grass. The two warriors turn to find Little-Bull and Blue-Leaf slowly making their way towards their position. Both were armed with a bow and a quiver of war arrows. Dangling from their sides were also flint stone tomahawks.

"I heard the call of No-Horns, so I will go to him. When our enemies can be seen I will give the signal to attack. Until then, stay still, for they do not yet know we are aware of their presence," Tall-Eagle said to the three warriors. He then silently made his way towards No-Horns.

As he slowly crept through the grass... Tall-Eagle kept his head low... trying to make himself invisible... being constantly aware of places for concealment should detection necessitated.

Guided by the faint light of the stars... Tall-Eagle made his way to No-Horns... where there too was darkness to shield him.

"I can see them, Tall-Eagle," No-Horns said as Tall-Eagle settled into a soft nestle of gentle grass. Again, Tall-Eagle searched the darkness... searching the shadows... all senses on full alert... yet his enemies remain unseen.

"I still cannot see," he admitted to No-Horns... still unable to pick out the living shadows of the enemy from the inanimate ones.

"Perhaps you should have left with the elders," Left-Wing whispered, startling both Tall-Eagle and No-Horns with his sudden appearance. No-Horns had to resist the impulse to yelp in fear.

Left-Wing was revered throughout the plains for his stealthiness. His uncanny ability to drift upon the wind in a manner so graceful as to render him almost a shadow himself.

Tall-Eagle could only smile to himself inwardly as he forced his heart too slow to a steady pace. "Where there is war, there is Left-Wing," he said to his young friend.

"This is true," Left-Wing responded as he scans the dark grassy void that yawned before them. "I had hoped for this moment. Now we can end their story once and for all."

Tall-Eagle said nothing. Instead, he wondered about the scouts that were supposed to be watching the Crow's camp... wondering if they were still alive... or felled victim to Crow's vengeance?

Tall-Eagle had to force such unanswerable questions from his mind so that he may focus on the matter at hand. Least he be the one to fall at the hands of their enemies.

Red-River laid silently in the tall grass... wreathed in shadows. He felt his lips tug into a grimace of a smile as he thought of himself as a predator in its natural environment... a shadow among shadows. He watched in Lakota campsite with predatory eyes... anxiously awaiting his moment to attack... anxiously awaiting his moment for vengeance. The warrior was acutely aware of the dangers inherited in such an attack... but he believes the plan is perfect in its simplicity and viciousness... he will strike the campsite with speed and brute force... taking it's inhabitants by complete surprise. He believes despite his injuries... he can still lead the Crow to victory.

He turned his eyes behind him... surveying the inky darkness with unblinking eyes. He knew his warriors were there in the darkness... eager for open war which lies ahead. He knew they too thirsted for the destruction of vengeance. He then looked back towards the camp. He wasn't foolish enough to believe the camp was without scouts... watchers... those who stood guard throughout the night. He found a place close to the campsite... a place of deep darkness. He knew this is where the scouts skulked in deep shadows. Again he felt his lips pull into a wolfish snarl.

His warriors clung tightly to the shadows as they made their way closer toward their intended target. The night had grown extremely still and unnaturally quiet. Only the sound of a lonely owl could be heard floating on the nighttime breeze. Tiny stars glittered and shimmered in the unending depths of space. He knew that soon the moon will appear... signaling the moment for all-out war.

He then thought of the warriors with him now... those that are eager for warfare. Throughout the bitter night came the sounds of the dying... the constant hacking and coughing up of blood. The rasping, struggling for breath and the painful moans of their brothers of war was still fresh in their minds. The carnage inflicted by the Sioux was fresh in their mind. A fresh wound that needed to be addressed.

His thoughts then turned away from his people and focused more on selfish pursuits.

He remembered childhood Legends of the Cherokee Nation in the Grand League of the Iroquois. He thought of how a single warrior had brought together the small and scattered tribes... forming a powerful and formidable Confederation of Mighty Warriors. He knew the names of these great leaders will be sung in songs of courage and bravery for over a thousand winters. He too wanted to take his place in history. But this was only half of the reason for being here.

He then thought of the unusual beauty of Bull's-Tail... the stranger from the faraway lands. Her name was derived from the texture of her hair... which was soft... yet course looking... like that of a buffalo's tail. His brother had found her wandering lost and alone... and claimed her as his bride. But in the deep recesses of his heart... he secretly wished it was he who had found her first. But he kept these treacherous emotions well hidden. It didn't take long before she tried escaping... forcing his brother, White-Chief, to placer in bondage. Secretly his heart rejoiced when she took White-Chief's life and escaped... for now according to Crow law her life belongs to White-Chief's next of kin. Now her life belongs to Red-River... he need only to claim it as his.

He didn't want to end her life, no. His mission was to break the woman's spirit... rendering her subordinate to his every whim.

But now these detestable snakes wish to deny him his right and pleasure.

His justification was the death of his brother... for his tribe understood he would certainly be single-minded in his pursuit of his brother's killer. But his true objective was Bull's-Tail... and he was no doubt willing to pursue this objective with no regard for the loss of life.

Slowly the moon mounted the nighttime sky. In the cold silver light of the moon, the sprawling grassy plain swayed in the breeze like a rippling sea. With a growing light, Red-River was now able to take in his immediate surroundings. Then with highly trained eyes, he worked his way out in calculated sectors. All the while fingering his bow in growing anticipation.

Suddenly... in the distance... he detected a glimpse of a living shadow... and then another, and then another. Dark anticipation shrouded his heart as he watched the descending figures turn into the dark shadows of men.

A shrill war-whoop split the air... the first omen of their impending death. Out of the darkness, arrows whistle menacingly as they rain dangerously close. Red-River let out his own war cry... signaling their own deadly attack.

Battle-cries filled the air as arrows fell from the heavens. Red-River released an arrow into the darkness... depending on sheer luck rather than skill. Nearby, to his right, he heard the agonizing cry as one of his warriors was struck. He turned in time to see the young warrior stumble to the ground... Withering and pain as he lay on his back ... his hands clasping at the arrow that was embedded in his stomach. He struggled for a moment and then he was quiet and still.

At least it was a quick death.

Red-River turned his attention back towards the camp. Just as he was pulling the sinew string taunts... he saw a shadow against the small campfire... a dark swift-moving shadow. He thought himself to be lucky... for now, he had a definitive target. Pulling the string with all his might... he aimed the arrowhead far above his target. The projectile was released with a quick reverberation as the arrow sailed murderously through the air. The arrow held steady and true... and it found it's mark. Above the whooping war-cries came the cry of agonizing pain as the arrow lodged itself deep into the warrior's chest. The wounded shadow fell into darkness.

Red-River personal victory was short-lived, for to his left fell another one of his warriors. The man fell on his back... a single arrow was buried halfway up it's shaft... protruding directly above his heart.

Red-River pulled another arrow from his quiver and search the plains for another target. And to his utter dismay... he saw with great dread as the Lakota begin a charge against his Crow warriors. He saw as they swarmed the grassy plains in an almost graceful manner. He let out another war-cry and released an arrow into the Lakota swarm. The arrow sailed harmlessly into the grass.

As he was reaching for yet another arrow, there was an abrupt burst of pain in his abdomen. Shocked, Red-River dropped his tools of war and slightly staggered in the grass. *Not again he,* thought gravely to himself as he found himself reaching blindly towards his stomach with questioning fingers.

There he had found blood seeping from a new wound... a wound mere inches from the old one... turning the bandages and his hands hot and sticky with blood. From the realization... the sharp pain returned to him in an agonizing wave that splintered his hope of emerging unscathed.

He gently caressed the arrow shaft that jolted from his abdomen.

All around him were the shrieking cries of war-whoops as the swiftly moving shadows engaged in war.

His vision grew blurry... remaining so for several seconds. Although the slightest physical exertion caused excruciating agony... he willed himself to remain focus... fighting back unconsciousness.

With his mind sharpen by the very instinct of self-preservation... he looked up to see his warriors already in a fervid flight to escape. The wounded warrior followed suit... staggering with every step he made... receding into the darkness of distance.

The initial Lakota enemy onslaught was a failure in the eyes of Tall-Eagle. Although he stood strong and proud... deep within, he felt his entire body trembling. He turned his gaze from the fleeing Crow to the moon filled sky... waiting patiently for the adrenaline to burn itself out. His hands shook slightly from the lethal encounter... but it was so subtle that not even well-trained eyes could measure its movements. All around him were the victory yelps of his warriors as they celebrated. A few of them gave chase... releasing arrows as they ran.

Quickly Tall-Eagle called them back... for through bitter experience he knew the warriors who gave chase could easily be running into an ambush.

The warriors returned at once.

He scanned the plains before him... the vast fields of grass looked lush and deceptively peaceful under the bright glow of the moon. His ears were open for any sound that disturbed the fragile integrity of the soft rustling grass. Towards the other side of the camp came whining neighs of startled horses. A single glance towards the direction of a younger boy sent the young warrior on his way to soothe the fretful beasts.

Again he looked towards the plains... and in the tall grass, he could see indentations. He saw two of them. Instinctively he knew bodies were the cause for these imprints. This caused them to think of his own warriors.

"No-Horns has been struck," Left-Wing said as if on some sadistic cue.

Tall-Eagle went to where Left-Wing stood above the fallen brave. In the bright light of the moon, the blood that wept from his chest wound seem dark and thick. With every breath No-Horns took, there was a faint wheezing... and an even softer gargle. They knew his lungs had been pierced... and is now filling with blood.

No-Horns face remained calm... knowing death was on the prowl... but accepting it without complaint in the fashion of a Lakota warrior.

Slow and low... Blue-Stalk began to sing the song of death... a warrior's chant reserved only for those who died in battle. The gathering warriors followed suit... each chanting in their own distinctive style.

Tall-Eagle felt himself blinking against the sting of unshed tears. His heart went out to the young brave... a brave of only 19 winters and never before had his voice heard in the council lodge. He watched as the brave painfully inhaled... then slowly exhaled for the last time. His face becoming peaceful and serene as he joined his People that went before him.

The gathering warriors finish their song then look towards Tall-Eagle. The leader felt the weight of their gaze upon him. He knew they were awaiting instructions.

Tall-Eagle knew they didn't have the Medicine-Man to conduct a proper burial. And time was against them, for now, they must follow the trail of In-The-Woods. But even if they did have the time and resources... it will be foolish to bury him with the infuriated Crow pursuing them... for these savages would no doubt desecrate the sacred burial site to satisfy their own barbarous quest for vengeance. But he knew taking No-Horns to his ancestral lands could jeopardize the remaining tribe... for it would slow them down exponentially.

He then thought of the Deer-Lady and how he, without second-guessing, escorted her on a pony-drag. No-Horns gave his life for the Deer-Lady. So a proper barrier and his ancestral Homeland is his by right. "Prepare to draw trios," he said to Big-Rock.

He then looked down upon the brave once again. And in this fallen warrior he began to see a dim and distant outline of the faith that may lay before them all. And although the vision wasn't perfect... uncertain... he knew that the fate of not only the Deer-Lady... but of his warriors laid in his hands.

"Let us rest while we can. At first light we break camp. This will give extra time for the Crow, who will need to conduct burial ceremonies," Tall-Eagle stated as he looked towards the two indentations. "Little-Bull and Left-Wing will stay with me to keep watch. The rest... sleep well, for we have a long and hard journey before us. Tell the Strange-One he may use my lodge if he wishes. We will protect him throughout the night. "

"He is gone" Yellow-Horse said. "In the heat of battle I watched him slip away."

Throughout the night, Tall-Eagle force himself to stay fully alert... keeping his every nerve strung to the highest point of tension. After a while he replaced Little-Bull and Left-Wing with Rising-Star and Red-Bear... the three sentinels prowling the surrounding area like predatory wolves... constantly on guard and protecting their pack. Before long, the eastern skies begin to pale... competing with the light of the moon. Soon the stars begin to fade and the gray light of the rising sun was slowly growing.

Tall-Eagle sent Red-Bear to awaken the camp. White-Sun and Mocking-Bird were already trying to bring the small fire back to life. They wanted to prepare a quick meal while the men prepared the camp for departure. Rising-Star went to prepare the horses. A cold chill from the morning's air penetrated his flesh and touch his very bones.

A shiver tore through his body.

Tall-Eagle repositioned his bow... an arrow hung loosely from the string. Slowly he made his way towards one of the indentations... a place he knew a fallen enemy laid. He knew his enemies will be watching the area... to ensure no-one desecrated their fallen. So the warrior stepped with true caution... his eyes constantly on the lookout.

The closest indentation to him embraced a man with an arrow lodged in his heart. He was laying on his back... stiff and rigid. On his face... a strange look of rage, and not fear, twisted his young features... his mouth contorted in a silent scream as he stared towards the heavens with unseeing eyes.

The second indentation was too far away. He thought it best to let it be and returned to camp.

The Mayan stranger awoke to the starkness of silence. Her wary body felt tight and tense as she clawed at the buffalo robe that embraced her... trying desperately to free her legs.

Her body was covered in sweat... and with the warmth of the small fire lodge... her naked flesh felt hot to the touch. She looked around at the lodge... trying desperately to remember where she was.

Instantly, her mind flashed back to the Crow and their savage brutality. Her heart pumped wildly in her chest as she looked around for a weapon... anything that could be used to protect herself.

As she stood... her legs trembled and shook... unable to support her weight. She stumbled back to the buffalo robe bed... her arms shaking as she supported her body.

Strenuously, she reached for a soft buckskin blanket to wrap around her naked frame. All the while her eyes continue to search for some sort of weapon.

None was found.

Suddenly, the flap of the lodge came open... and in the round hole appear a woman. The two startle each other as they stood looking at each other.

The Mayan stranger felt the chill from outside. And as she looked beyond the Sioux woman... she could see many men walking about the camp... each one of them banishing some sort of weapon.

Full-fledged panic struck the Mayan stranger as she thought about the Crow she had murdered. And in her heart, she knew only her life could repay the debt she had created with such an act. She knew she had to escape before they bound her again.

The Mayan stranger let out a soft whimper as she rose to her feet... her eyes as wild and wary as a trapped animal. The Sioux said nothing... she merely watched as the Mayan stumbled forward... slowly gathering strength as she did. Once at the door, she pushed at the Sioux woman with all the strength she could muster... but her thin build had little impact on the woman's powerful build.

Even so, the woman stepped aside... allowing the Mayan to stumble out into the bright early morning ... landing in grass that was wet with dew.

Although the sun was but low in the eastern sky... she still had to shut her eyes against its harsh glare. The morning air hit her sweaty body with a forceful chill. She looked up and saw that the campsite was crawling with activities. They all seem quiet and grim-faced. The heavy cold seemed to be dampening most of the movements so that they worked in eerie silence.

Fear drove her as she got to her feet... one hand held steadily before her while the other held the buckskin blanket close. She stumbled into what had to be the center of the camp, and all around her were fully dressed warriors. Now all eyes were on her.

Her soft brown eyes were wide and troubled as she looked about her... searching each face for some hint of hope... or even reassurance. None of the warriors moved. They only looked upon her in silence.

From behind her a pair of arms encircled her... but it wasn't forceful and she easily broke free from the grip. Turning around she found herself looking into the eyes of another woman. "Leave me alone," the Mayan snarled furiously in a language unknown to the Sioux woman. And although she injected anger into her voice... it still shook with fear.

After breaking loose, the Mayan again searched for a weapon. And there... littering the ground like a promise of salvation, laid numerous arrows.

She swept her hand over the wet grass... grabbing an arrow. She then turned on the woman... holding the flint-tipped arrow before her as a weapon.

Suddenly, a lone warrior stood before her... his size and structure immediately dwarfing the tall, yet fragile woman. As she looked into his eyes... she found no warmth in them. Instead... his dark eyes seem to regard her as a hunter would regard as prey. He then reached to the small of his back and produced a flint knife. An evil grin seemed to play over his lips as she stared frightfully at the outstretched arm.

The first woman quickly approached the large man and forcefully shoved aside the knife. The man then smiled mischievously at the woman. This invoked a laugh from the men that now surrounded her. He said something to her in a strange language... only to be forcefully rebutted by the much shorter woman. The man lowered his head in mock shame and left. At his departure, she turned back towards the Mayan.

Her hand continued to tremble as she held the arrow in her grip. And although the short woman may have just saved her... she still thrust the arrow towards her the moment she took a step forward. "Don't come any closer," she said in her Mayan language... her voice trembling with emotion... praying against prayer that woman would take heed to her warning. She didn't want to... but she was willing to strike again if it meant her staying free.

"Tall-Eagle!" Left-Wing shouted as he quickly approached the acting Chief. "The woman, the Deer-Lady, she has risen and is now holding White-Sun hostage," he said as he chuckled to himself.

Tall-Eagle was well aware of Left-Wing's dark humor... so he wondered if there were any truth in his words. It was then did he notice that Left-Wing had his knife in hand. "Why the Weapon?" he asked inquisitively.

"Crow," Left-Wing said as he smiled. "Are we not at war?"

"That we are. Where is the Deer-Lady? "

"She is towards the center. Just follow the crowd."

With that being said, Tall-Eagle turned to find her. And as he was walking away, Left-Wing said "Listen not to White-Sun, for she wishes only to get me into trouble." Tall-Eagle didn't respond... instead, he sighed softly to himself... wondering what his young friend had done now.

Tall-Eagles saw the gathering crowd that Left-Wing had spoken about. And in the center was the Deer-Lady... and in her quivering hand she held a Crow's arrow. White-Sun was indeed trying to talk the Deer-Lady down... but he could tell by the wild look in her eye that it was to no avail.

Slowly, Tall-Eagle stepped in between the two... and the Deer-Lady looked up at him. And at that very moment, he thought that her frightened face and wild eyes had never looked more deer-like or full of wild beauty.

With what seemed like great effort she finally was able to focus her eyes on him. Yet some of that wild look remained. But he could feel how desperately she wanted to trust somebody. He could also sense how terrified she was of doing just that.

He took a small, tentative step towards her... and in desperation she thrust the arrow towards him in a threatening manner. But the warrior held fast... taking another tentative step forward. Again she held up the weapon... saying something in that strange language. It was then did he realize how husky her voice was. And in that husky voice was a world of raw anger and bitterness. And even more... in her voice was an underlying desire to trust someone... anyone. A subtle cry for help that she could not voice... or was afraid to do so. The desire was quite subtle... but Tall-Eagle could feel it.

"With us you are well protected," he said quite softly... well aware that she was hearing tones more than words. "Know that I will protect you."

The Mayan looked around at the warriors that surrounded her. She then looked up at Tall-Eagle with pain-filled eyes. Again she said something in that strange language... but this time it was spoken softly... a mere whisper as she stared at him with an expression of hopeless desire. An expression that tugged at the strings of his heart once again.

The hand that held up the buckskin blanket began to shake as badly as the hand that possessed the arrow.

Tall-Eagle took another small step towards her. The Mayan did not move. Slowly he took another step forward... whispering ever so softly as he did so. And soon he had encircled his hands around the hand that held the weapon... his large and rough hands becoming soft and gentle. Her shaking hand felt so small in his clasp... her fingers trembling in his grip like a captured bird. As he removed the weapon from her hand she said something more... something with a small pleading note in her voice.

It was more than the Mayan woman could bear. Unable to control the onslaught of adrenaline that continued to pump through her... her chest grew tight and her breath became dangerously thin. Her legs then buckled and her eyes rolled towards the back of her head. And once again the Mayan found herself falling into the realm of unconsciousness.

Tall-Eagle moved in quickly to catch her in his powerful arms... then slowly lowered her to the ground.

"She sleeps yet again," Left-Wing announced loudly to the crowd, expecting the laugh. But none came. "We fight for her while she sleeps."

White-Sun shot Left-Wing a dirty look. But it did little to dissuade his need for a laugh. She quickly approached the fallen Mayan and Tall-Eagle. After looking over the woman she said, "It is true, she sleeps. The excitement was too much for her. But now we know that she is healthy."

"And crazy," Left-Wing stated in pursuit of a laugh. One he finally received.

Tall-Eagle could feel the sleeping woman shivering... so he placed an arm about her in an attempt to keep her from the chill of the early morning.

"Take her back to my Lodge," White-Sun instructed Tall-Eagle. He picked her up gently... being careful to keep the buckskin blanket in place. He then carried her to the lodge of White-Sun.

The wounded Crow felt the horse's complex coordination of hard muscle working as he laid upon his back... grasping on to his mane. Unable to sit up due to the pain... Red-River could only grimace in pain as the great creature carried him to safety.

The horse came upon a river, then slowed it's pace. The morning sun glistened off the rippling currents as they nibbled hungrily at the shore. Slowly and painfully, the injured warrior dropped from his horse and made his way to the riverbank... a place where the moss-covered rocks felt slippery and lazy swirling swarms of insects hovered just beyond the water's edge. Towards the center of the dark water was drift-wood that bobbed as it was swept downstream.

Red-River drop to a knee and dipped his cupped hands into the rushing clear water. And there he drank... sighing after each handful. For a moment he began to wonder what it was that had led him to this point. And above all... he began to wonder if it was worth the pain. And it was that pain that threatened to break his iron resolve... the resolve of retrieving Bull's-Tail.

With wet fingers, he probed at his bandages. And there he found the broken shaft of a Lakota's arrow protruding from his stomach. A mixture of pain and anger surged through him as he tried pulling the arrow bit from his flesh. But it was more than he could bear.

Behind him, he heard the sound of an approaching horse. Share panic threatened to overtake him as he jumped to his feet... But the sharp pain in his side greatly outweighed whatever panic may have come... and once again his injury became the singular focal point of his attention.

"Red-River!" a familiar voice called out. "We thought you were lost to us. How great is it that you still live?"

The wounded warriors looked up at the approaching Crow... and because the rider and his horse was coming from the east... the morning sun was at their backs. Red-River had to shield his eyes from the harsh glare as the horse stopped just before him. "Indeed, I live. Despite the fact that I was abandoned," he fumed silently... but his words carry undeniable weight.

"We were overwhelmed," the Crow called Blue-Raven protested.

"Many were struck. We needed to retreat in order to regroup and to strategize."

Red-River said nothing more on the subject. Instead, he dropped his loincloth and stood naked just before the river's edge. Cautiously, he wadded out towards the dark middle... but he didn't go far... for soon the rushing water was up to his chest... completely submerging his wounds. The icy-cold current curled and glide around his wide chest... draining the heat of battle from his body. The cold water greatly reduced the pain of his injuries... but he knew more will be needed.

All around them was the never-ending sea of grass... tall and turning green... always waving and rippling in the constant wind. But within the field of grass were pockets of colors... the colors of flowers. Red ones... white ones... purple ones... blue ones... and he knew which ones could be eaten. But more importantly... he knew which ones made good medicine.

"Find me the purple coneflower and bring it to me," Red-River said sternly.

Blue-Raven looked out towards Red-River... the sun glistening off the running water around him. "Shall I gather the others first? They wait just beyond that hill," he said as he pointed towards the rising sun.

"Bring me the purple coneflower," he repeated... his tone was as hard as flint. Both Red-River and Blue-Raven knew that the root of the flower was used to greatly dull pain. And it was the forcefulness of Red-River tone that told Blue-Raven how great his pain actually was. Without another word being spoken... he turned his horse from the river in search of the flower. Once again Red-River was left alone with his thoughts. And once again his thoughts gravitated towards the beauty of the Mayan woman.

High above, the heavens was still red as the burning light of the morning sun partially hid behind fluffy floating clouds. In a low and hesitating voice, he began to chant a war song. A song where the singer was defeated in battle... a song where the singer swears vengeance and would not find rest until retribution was gained.

Slowly the words of his chant grew clearer and stronger. As he pulled the bandages from his body... his voice grew louder... growing in power at the strength of his conviction. Soon he had the strength and conviction to pull the arrow tip from his numbing flesh.

The oath of vengeance came from deep within Red-River... a place he believed the magic and power of his convictions flows in its most primitive form.

The power of his song attracted the attention of a red-tail hawk. The mighty bird circled lazily overhead as it sang its own song. Seeing this as a good omen... Red-River began to send his song to the heavens in pursuit of the great bird-of-prey.

Blue-Raven returned to the riverbank... in hand he held the root. Red-River made his way to the shore... then step from the icy water onto the bank. The water fell freely from his naked body as a violent shiver tore through him. The blood-soaked bandages had been removed while his body was submerged... but still, the wounded wept freely... blood mixing with the water as it ran the length of his body.

Red-River took the root from Blue-Raven and begin to chew on it... the bitterness causing his mouth too greatly water. Once the root became paste-like... he plugged his wound and tied a strip of his leggings around him like a second bandage.

After dressing he climbed back upon his horse... ready to ride. The pain was still there... and the pain was still great. But the anger that scalded his heart fought against the pain... and he was ready to return to the warriors that fought under him. Ready to return them to the Lakota campsite for a second battle.

Tall-Eagle set up on his horse... gazing towards the lands in the West. A gentle wind caressed his face. The same wind that played in the prairie grass... causing it to billow in rhythmic waves like the sea... rolling and rippling the vastness until it touched the heavens in the distance. In the sky... blue clouds cast grey shadows upon the grass... each shadow racing one another over the fields like colossal eagles with spread wings.

All about him were men working tirelessly. With swift hands and strong arms, they made quick work of breaking down the camp and preparing the horses... and soon they will depart. The acting chief knew they would be moving through territories claimed by several tribes... where each tribe held varying loyalties. Even so, most of his attention had been absorbed by the Mayan stranger and her stark beauty. Many a time he has seen her as she slept. But it wasn't quite the same as seen such beauty and motion.

He couldn't help but to look upon the Mayan with sympathetic pity. Even so... her face was thin and protruding... and her hair was wild. Slender and tall she was in that Buffalo robe, but it seemed she had an inner strength about her... an inner strength that was as hard as flint. Perhaps she is the daughter of Kings... the offspring of gods as the Strange-One has said. To see her for the first time in the full light of day... to see her in all her beauty... it caused his mind to wander.

And then there were her eyes. By the spirit that dwells in all... those big brown eyes... resembling pools of honey when in sunlight. And there... in the mist was a sad desperation... a kind of rage at life and the cruelty of it. It was as if through her eyes he could feel her thoughts... reaching towards him... grasping at his soul. Wanting so desperately to trust him.

"The time has come, Tall-Eagle," came a soft-spoken voice... as if not wanting to interrupt his thoughts.

The acting Chief turned to find Pretty-Elk upon his own steed. And behind him were the rest of his warriors. Each one upon his own horse... and each horse carry in its own type of tiresome burden. The full weight of the camp was now upon the horse's back.

"Both No-Horns and the stranger were positioned towards the center. Protected at both ends," Pretty-Elk said.

A slow, but burning red began to creep into the cheeks of Tall-Eagle. A slow anger caused by the fact that somehow he had momentarily forgotten about the death of his youngest warrior. How easy it has become to forget about the important things when in the presence of the Mayan.

He knew he had to stay focused.

With a motion of a hand, two of his warriors went ahead of the group. They will be the scouts for the first leg of the journey. And one by one each man fell into line... guiding the horses with but a spoken word. Soon White-Sun and Mocking-Bird fell into place. The acting Medicine-Woman was dragging the body of No-Horns and her young apprentice carried the sleeping Mayan.

The sudden movement of Mocking-Bird's horse must have jarred the Mayan from her sleep... for in a quick instant she was up, and once again scared for her life.

Tall-Eagle's horse leapt to life as he guided it towards the frightened woman. A frightened woman who quickly found herself surrounded by warriors. Once again she found herself searching her immediate surroundings for a weapon.

Reading her thoughts, Left-Wings taunt body jerked into swift action... seizing her by the wrist in an iron grip. With little effort, he slung her to the ground. Like a predatory animal, he slowly walked towards her... producing a flint knife as he did so.

The Mayan's eyes fell upon the blade... it was long and heavy... with a deadly look. It was the same man who had threatened her before. A violent shiver tour through her as she thought of what is in store.

White-Sun had reached Left-Wing before Tall-Eagle did... And again the woman was scolding him for his childish antics. "Can you not see how frightened she is? Why must you always play?" flashed White-Sun scornfully at Left-Wing.

"She threatened my life. I am the one in fear," Left-Wing responded. But all games ceased with the arrival of Tall-Eagle.

Tall-Eagle leapt from his moving horse and stepped towards the commotion. He shot Left-Wing and icy glare... but Left-Wings eyes danced with mischief as he smiled amusingly at his own boyish eagerness for trouble.

Turning towards the Mayan, Tall-Eagle saw that her eyes were glued to the weapon Left-Wing held in his hand. "Leave us," he ordered his warrior, his voice hard and stern. Left-Wing says something with slow, deliberate sarcasm... but still did as he was instructed.

"Shhhh," White-Sun whispered softly... trying to soothe the Mayan.

Tall-Eagle stepped forward. And it was then that their eyes truly met for the first time.

She remembered him. She remembered how he sat upon his horse as she laid next to the dead Crow. She grasped his role... slowly... only by degrees. And soon she had become to realize that he had saved her. She wanted so desperately to relax... but knew that there is always something evil lurking just beneath the surface of man.

Even so... her eyes took the man's measure in a single glance. He was tall... handsome and much younger than her. His luxurious hair gathered in full plats that fell down his back. He had a wild and free look to him. And he stared at her with eyes that held hers with a feverish intensity. There was a world of emotions in there... but mostly the sadness that lurked in his eyes begged her for her trust. She knew not what to do.

She looked around for the first man. In a flash, she knew he was trouble... for she had learned to recognize what is dangerous in man. And his actions were that of a mischievous man... a forceful man. Very dangerous to encounter. She felt her pulse heightened as she thought of him.

Her attention was brought back to the man that stood before her. With gentle persuasion, he says something in a strange language. His voice was calm... soothing.

"Please do not harm me," she whispered ever-so-softly in her Mayan language. She knew there was a language barrier between the two... but she was trying to speak to the spirit more than anything.

Tall-Eagle took another small step towards the Mayan. She whispered again in that strange language. There was so much pain in her voice. He took another step towards her. He caught a slight quivering of her frame... her eyes danced of desperation.

He could tell her muscles had not gotten accustomed to movement. She had been unconscious for two days. "Bring some water," he said to nobody in particular. It was Mocking-Bird who responded.

With water and hand, Tall-Eagle took yet another small step towards the Mayan. He poured some of the liquid onto his hand and held it up. A beam of the low sun-light through parting clouds fell upon his wet hand... causing it to glisten invitingly.

The stranger licked her dry lips with and even drier tongue. She started to step forward. The woman hesitated again... truly wary as a wild deer. She couldn't help but to voice the question in her soft eyes as he looked at Tall-Eagle. And Tall-Eagle nodded knowingly towards her. So with lingering traces of fear, she gave way to the thirst and reached for the bag of water.

The first gulps of water she took went down her chin. She continued to stare at Tall-Eagle as she drank. Her hair was wild and three or four locs hung over her forehead.

"Slowly," he whispered to her, placing a steady hand on her neck and shoulders.

Never had she had water that tasted so good. She could literally feel the soothing longitude spreading throughout her body. The tension seemed to drain from her as she drank.

The man says something in his native tongue... his voice thick with emotion. And as he spoke, he placed a warm hand upon her fragile shoulder. Only then did she realize how cold it was... her breath was almost visible before her. Her shoulders were bare... the buffalo robe that was wrapped around her stopped just beneath her arms. But the warmth of his touch had spread a calming wave over her entire body. A kind of warmth she knew could come only from an earnest spirit.

Slowly she handed the water back to the man and bowed her head slightly in a gesture of thanks. The younger woman stepped forward to retrieve the water. Unlike the older woman, she had a fine built to herself. Not robust... yet full and strong, and very capable of handling life's heavy demands.

Again she looked about herself. All around her were warriors. Each one just as young as the next. She had become the single focal point of their fascination, and they simply stared at her like solemn owls... wide-eyed and quiet. And again she began to feel uneasy... until she returned her gaze to the man that stood before.

His eyes seemed to lift her out of her weakness... to fill her with a sort of comfort that swept away all fears... all doubts... all troubles. And for at least that very moment... she began to feel at ease.

But the moment was instantly shattered as that bad man with the knife quickly approached. He was seething in anger... his voice full of hostility. Immediately she was filled with dread. She wanted to leave.

He says something to the man that stood before her, gesturing with his hand. To her, his moves were threatening. Where this threat was directed towards... she could not tell. But it incidentally affected the entire group of warriors.

Oh, how she wish he would leave. She wanted that fleeing moment to return. She needed that moment to return. Just to restore her to sanity.

"The Crows have returned!" Left-Wing stated gravely as he approached Tall-Eagle, pointing towards the east with his flint knife.

Tall-Eagle turned a cold glance suddenly upon the distant hills. And there... across the lush valley atop of hill stood three horsemen. The light from the low sun illuminated their profiles in an eerie fashion.

Instinctively he knew more riders were on the other side of the hill... hidden from view.

He turned to retrieve his horse, but a pair of hands collapsed around his arm. It was the Mayan... the Deer-Lady. She had literally shrank away from Left-Wing... trying to hide behind Tall-Eagle like a child... eyeing Left-Wing suspiciously.

Deep within... he felt the over-powering need to protector her. But still, he had to pull away.

In a single stride, Tall-Eagle was upon his horse... and the animal leapt to life willingly beneath him. But before he rode off he took one last glance back at the Deer-Lady. White-Sun was speaking soothingly to her... trying to adjust the Mayans robe. The look in her eyes returned to it's grave and wary gaze. Even so... they were blinking back the tears as she gained a small measure of composure and allowed herself to be dragged away.

Tall-Eagle had instructed the tribe to start moving again... he knew the enemy Crow were becoming anxious to collect their dead.

Slowly the line of Lakota moved forward... a line that wound in and out of view along the game trail... traveling towards the way of the setting sun. The vast prairie stretched endlessly before them. As they traveled, each person remained silent... lost in their own thoughts.

Tall-Eagle had allowed the Mayan to take his horse and he walked beside the two. At first, he was unable to keep his eyes off this beautiful Mayan, and she became uncomfortably aware of this. He would look up at her... absorbing the beauty and elegance of her odd face... her frail build... unable to ward off the building emotions he felt blossoming into a type of kinship with her vulnerability.

As the group solemnly strolled forward, Tall-Eagle kept a watchful gaze upon the Crow... the Crow who were careful to keep their distance. They were nothing more than mere specks upon the landscape.

The sun had continued its celestial journey across the deep heavens... it's radiant fingers gently caressing the long sweeping grass that swayed under the constant breeze. The warmth of the sun fought valiantly against the spring breeze that touched his flesh. He knew that soon he would have to stop to make camp. He summoned two warriors,

Brave-Shield and Turns-Black, and instructed them to ride ahead seeking a place for refuge.

Before long, Left-Wing guided his horse towards the acting chief. "Has she spoken?" he asked as he looked down upon the walking Tall-Eagle.

"She has not," he said simply.

"What is your name?" Left-Wing ask the Mayan in the Dakota language.

She looked across at the mean-spirited warrior. The mischievous and lazy grin that crept across his thin lips made her feel uncomfortable. She didn't look down at the one walking beside her.

Tall-Eagle saw the fear had crept back into her eyes... eyes that reached out to him.

"What is your name?" repeated the question softly, this time in the Crow language. When she didn't respond, Left-Wing asked the same question in four other languages, none of which receive an answer.

"Well," he said to Tall-Eagle, "this is the extent of my knowledge of other languages. You've attended more councils than me. Councils from tribes far and wide. Perhaps you'll find a common language."

Tall-Eagle knew there was wisdom in Left-Wings words. But of all the people, of all the lands, never has he seen a people which resembles this Deer-Lady. As much as he despised the Crow... their women were strangely beautiful. They, too, are thin. But they lack the height of the Deer-Lady. But it's her hair... the softness... the texture... this is what sets her apart from any woman he has ever encountered. And her eyes. Eyes that seemed to swirl like honey in a dark gaze which held a singular magnetic power over this season Warrior. All so confusing to him.

After Left-Wing checked his horse and led it in the direction of which the group traveled, Tall-Eagle looked up at the Mayan. The Mayan looked coyly at the acting chief as she once again took small nipples from a berry-cake.

"If only you can understand my words," he said in Cherokee.

The Mayan lowered her eyes... as if to deal with some unspoken emotions. Again she took a small bite from the cake patty. Slowly she chewed the dried berries. "I understood your friend," the Maya said in a broken Hopi dialect.

The acting chief was taken completely by surprise. His people had traded with the Hopi for many generations. He has sat in on these trades for as long as he could remember. But she didn't resemble any Hopi woman he had ever encountered. The Hopi people were very small, and sunburned from living within the Great-Sands. How did this Mayan come to speak this language?

Barely able to control the excitement within, he anxiously asked, "Why did you not respond before?"

"Your friend," she said as she gestured with her chin towards the direction of Left-Wing, "I have encountered men like him before. I do not wish to speak to him."

"Left-Wing is our finest warrior," he assured the Mayan. "His heart is righteous." He then paused, trying to choose his words carefully. "Upon first encounter, one would assume his heart is callous. Without Love. Without passion. But I assure you, I will put my life in his hands before any other man."

The two then fell into a deep silence. Tall-Eagle wanted so desperately to speak to her. There were so many questions to ask. But he feared appearing too eager.

"Thank you," the Deer-Lady says suddenly, breaking Tall-Eagle's train of thought. He had to resist the overpowering urge to bombard her with questions, with words, with conversation. Instead, he simply bowed his head and continue to guide the horse in silence. Before long, Turns-Black returned with news of a suitable campsite for the band.

"It's upon a grand hill, with nothing obstructing the view," he had informed Tall-Eagle. "But we must hasten our pace if we wish to make it."

"Ride ahead with Brave-Shield and Blue-Leaf so that buffalo dung may be gathered for fires," Tall-Eagle instructed. As swift as arrows in the wind, the young braves and the horses were adrift on the breeze. He then glanced at the Mayan, and etched within her liquid brown doe-eyes was a lurking fear.

"Is it them?" she asked in the Hopi language. "Is it the people who wish to do me harm?" the fear in her voice raked across his hearts with cold fingers. He wondered what it was that she had suffered at the hands of the evil and wicked Crow.

"You have nothing to fear. My Scouts had just informed me of a place for us to rest tonight. They rode ahead to prepare for our arrival." He then fell into an uneasy silence. Finally said, "I am Tall-Eagle. We are the Little-Star-Band, a People from the Lakota Nation."

He paused, awaiting a response from the Deer-Lady. She seemed unwilling to meet his gaze. So he continued, "We just broke winter's cap. Now we seek the buffalo herds."

The Mayan simply sat upon the guided horse. Her head was slightly bowed, her hands clasping tightly to the horse's mane. Every so often she would have raised her eyes to look at Tall-Eagle, but she would quickly avert her gaze.

They rode some time in silence, the Little-Star-Band riding in stoic silence, while their horse's hooves fell silently upon the prairie grass. Only the soft swishing of the endless grass was a constant... periodically broken by the neigh of a horse.

"Is it true that you are Mayan? A descendant of those who dwell in stone cities that reach the heavens?" he finally asked. He made sure his voice didn't betray any of the wanting emotions he felt energized in him.

"These are such stories that are told to the young. But I have been told, by a wise traveler, that these stone pyramids are real."

Again, the Deer-Lady didn't respond. And for a brief moment, he began to question his sanity. He began to wonder if she has spoken to him at all. Or perhaps his Hopi wasn't as well-spoken as he believed?

"I am a Mayan," she said suddenly, "From the conquered city of Perez. But our buildings do not touch the heavens." She then fell back into a heavy silence.

"And your name?" he gently prodded, looking up at her with the softest look this season warriors could muster.

"My true name has been stolen. Stolen by the Spanish conquistadors. Stolen by those who first struck us with illness. Then slaughtered those few who survived."

There was a world of sadness in her husky voice. Oh, how he wish he could take the pain away from this beautiful woman. "I have many names. Everywhere I travel, people always give me a new name.

At this revelation, Tall-Eagle begin to laugh. A laughter that caused the Mayan to feel self-conscious. She quickly lowered her head and fell back into a deep silence. "I laughed not at you, my Mayan friend. I laughed because my people believe you resemble a deer. So they've been calling you the Deer-Lady. As well as the Mayan. Two new names to add to the many. So tell me, what is your name?"

"My name means Pretty in the Spanish language. My name is Linda. "

"Well, Linda, from the city of Perez, know that I would do all I can to ensure you remain safe."

Before long, the rolling hills came into view. Soon they will arrive at their new but temporal camping grounds. Tall-Eagle kept an eye on the pursuing Crow. But the Crow was lost in the gathering shadows as night gathered in the east. The endless prairies, clad with endless shades of green, now lay gray and eerie and the gathering twilight.

Finally, the band reached its destination. The grounds were already dim against the darkening sky. Tiny flames from small fires could barely be seen by the approaching band. The air was sweet... intoxicating as the smell of venison drifted towards them on the evening breeze.

Tall-Eagle smiled to himself with pride. His men were such fine warriors. Not only had they secured a safe spot for the night, they also made a successful kill and was already preparing its meat for their arrival.

Without being instructed, the horse watchers helped unload the horses, then gather them so that they may be cared for. White-Sun and Mocking-Bird finish preparing the venison as the rest hastily erected temporary shelters for the night.

The Mayan moved very little as the band settled in. Tall-Eagle stayed in constant motion... moving all about the camp to ensure everything was in order... her eyes watching his every move.

White-Sun had rationed the meat, ensuring all had their fair share. But the Mayan didn't eat. The pemmican and dry berry cakes she had eaten on the journey had serviced. Tall-Eagle took but a couple of bites before giving the rest to the eager Brave-Shield. There was a forced laughter amongst the band, for despite his small stature, Brave-Shield, was known for his insatiable hunger.

The young moon was shining, cold and gray, down upon the prairie. All around them, the grassy knolls and rounded hills took on a ghostly hue while the shadows of brush laid black.

Tall-Eagle and White-Sun approached the Mayan. "You will stay in the lodge of White-Sun," he told the Deer-Lady. "She doesn't speak Hopi. But she is very wise and can interpret if you were to sign. That's if you don't require anything further."

Within the growing shadows of the night, the black pools of his eyes sparkled with ethereal energy. He spoke softly... as if speaking to a child. Although she knew he meant well, for she could read the truth in his eyes, she couldn't help but feel slightly berated.

"I require nothing more," she responded in her husky voice. She instantly regretted it.

Tall-Eagle glanced at the Mayan, surprised... then said shyly, "May the spirits bring you pleasant dreams."

The Deer-Lady saw a twinge of sadness and those dark eyes. But before she could speak further, he turned and was gone. He became a shadow amongst moving shadows.

White-Sun took the Mayan by the hand and led her to a lodge. Once there she gently pushed the Mayan towards the door. "Go," she said in Lakota, knowing the Mayan would understand her gestures more than her words.

The Deer-Lady looked around one last time for Tall-Eagle. She wanted to catch one last glimpse at the one who has saved her from the dreadful Crow. She wanted so desperately to open up to him. But she knew she had to remain guarded. She knew the beastial violence of men all too well. Even the Crow, White-Chief, had been cordial in the beginning. While trading with the Hopi, White-Chief had lured the Mayan to follow him with false generosity and charms.

Already she was lost and alone. She didn't belong with a Hopi. When her village was utterly destroyed by the Spanish conquistadors, she knew not where to go... as the sole survivor she followed the old trading trails... trails that lead from the Mayan pyramids to the Hopi people.

Tall-Eagle took the first watch. His posts sat facing east... the direction of the pursuing Crow. The silver moon had risen beyond the earth's edge... rising up to defeat the darkness of the encroaching night; it's cold light bleaching the rolling hills with silvery light. The stars were hidden beyond grayish rain clouds... clouds that caught the light of the moon as well, given off a freakish grey-glow that laid in stark contrast against the black sky.

He knew that soon there will be a dreadful down poor... the heavens were building its watery army. He began to wonder if he could get his people to the land of the Yankton or Oglala before this celestial storm occurred. Already his horses and Band grow weary. The heavy burden of rain-soaked gear may completely break their horses.

He wrapped the buffalo blanket more tightly about his tight shoulders. The night had grown considerably cold. Tall-Eagle considered this a blessing, for the chill of the night added to his alertness. He was a seasoned warrior... a warrior that has spent countless other nights under the open sky as a scout. But this new wakefulness was deepened by the Crow threat.

From the heights of the hill, Tall-Eagle had an easy view of the neighboring hills. One would have to cover a great distance to reach their camp sight unseen. Indeed has scouts had done well.

The night was quiet. He could hear their horses munching on the tough prairie grass while a few wolves howled mournfully off in the distance. He knew what would come next. His heart grew heavy and sad incidentally... for it would always happen this time of night.

His thoughts turned towards Girl-Lost.

Always, during these lonely hours... during the most vulnerable time... he will sit and listen to the lonesome moan of the prairie wind...

listening to the mournful cry of wolves... listening to the playful yelps of young coyotes... and all these sad sounds became a part of his lonely existence. Oh, how he missed his Girl-Lost... his Gypsy-Angel. He had nothing left of her... nothing more than sad memories that would come to torture his imagination.

He forced himself to think of the situation at hand. He had three other scouts posted in the other three cardinal directions. He began to wonder what came to marr their imaginations this time of night. At the thought, he couldn't help but to laugh at himself. He and he alone possessed this innate weakness... the inability to let go of the past. No doubt the other warrior's minds will be running amuck with fantasies concerning the glories of war against the Crow. In their fevered minds they were already counting coup.

A genuine smile crept upon his lips.

Naturally, his mind slowly made his way to the Deer-Lady. How lucky he felt that the two could now communicate. Again, he felt his lips pull into a grin as he thought of the old man, the Strange-One, who claimed this Mayan was the descendants of ancient gods and goddesses. He would ask if this was true when the sun arrives in the morning. That and so many other things.

Suddenly, his muscles tighten with a rush of adrenaline as his peripheral registered a moving shadow.

Slowly and methodically he lowered himself to the grass. Slipping from beneath the buffalo robe, he gathered his bow and arrow. He narrowed his vision towards the position of the shadow. He saw nothing. But he knew a seasoned warrior could stay frozen in the same spot for quite a long time... awaiting the perfect opportunity to either strike or advance.

Tall-Eagle lowered himself onto his stomach. He knew it would be very difficult to fire an arrow from this position... but he wanted to crawl in the general direction... perhaps even surprising the surprise attacker.

With his every muscle tight and ready to spring into action... he slowly began to crawl... adrenaline pumping its volatile mixture throughout his taunt body. Like a wild cat stalking its prey through the glade, he slowly inched his way forward... his eyes staring intensely at his target.

That's when he saw a second shadow... a smaller shadow that stayed awfully close to the ground. He then saw a slight movement from the first shadow. Then all became deadly silent and calm. Tall-Eagle was barely able to see the supine shapes laying under the soft grass.

Slowly, Tall-Eagle got into a firing position, crouching on one knee. His back was still hunched as he tried to remain a part of the shadowy landscape. He then fitted an arrow and leveled its tip directly at one of the stilled shadows.

In the distance, he heard the blood curdling, yet beautiful bay of a wolf. At the sound, the two shadows stirred within its nest of darkness. A moment later, both shadows raise their heads and released their own mournful cries in unison. The two shadows then began to trot away... receding into the darkness.

Instantly, the rush of adrenaline began to dissipate... leaving him shaking with a mixture of angry-anticipation and intense relief.

The Mayan was awakened by a soft rustling made by White-Sun. She felt as if she had just conquered sleep when she was startled into full alertness. She laid with her eyes wide open... momentarily confused as to where she was. There was a small cooking fire within the tipi of what she laid... the light of its flames playing upon its walls with lights and shadows.

Slowly, her predicament began to set in as she remembered her situation.

Outside of the tipi, she heard more rustling, along with soft voices. She laid perfectly still, not wanting the other woman to know she slept no longer. Already, these people made her feel awkward. She was a complete stranger here. But she had always been a stranger no matter where she traveled. Ever since she narrowly escaped the dreadful fate of her people, she no longer belonged anywhere. Everywhere she went, she was a stranger... an outcast... a social misfit that didn't belong. No wonder White-Chief had little difficulties leading her away from the Hopi with empty promises and fake charm.

But again... She had nothing with the Hopi people. They shared nothing but a language. A strange language that she fought gallantly to master, for she knew this foreign language would be the only bond she shared with these people. But it was a bond she gratefully accepted.

Her thoughts were interrupted by the sound of White-Sun exiting the lodge. Once she was alone, she sat up to look around. The lodge was nearly empty, save a couple of bundles located near the door. The small flames spattered and crackled softly as it gave off a soft glow.

Suddenly, the door flat open and White-Sun appeared. The Mayan childishly try to flop back onto the ground to play sleep. But the Lakota woman had seen her.

The Lakota woman said something in her native tongue... but the Mayan continue to play sleep. Again the Lakota spoke, this time in a more scolding manner. But the Mayan refused to give up the ruse, for now, the awkwardness had grown exponentially. And if she admitted to faking asleep... it would only increase. So she laid as perfectly still and quiet as the dead... but the tightness of her eyes were a dead giveaway to the Lakota.

Her voice became somewhat hostile as she poked the Mayan in her rib cage. Despite her appearance... The Deer-Lady was far from fragile. The cruel fate that had been forced upon her had been like a flame that strengthened the shaft of an arrow. But the squat and powerfully built Lakota woman had fingers like buffalo horns. The Mayan couldn't help but to yelp and pain.

At that moment, the gig would have been up for the average person. But not to a determined woman who desperately wanted to avoid any awkwardness.

Slowly, the Mayan raised to an elbow as if aroused from a deep sleep. She rose with a yawn and a stretch... gently rubbing her eyes. "Huh?" She said softly as she looked at the scrawling Lakota with the most innocent face she can muster.

In the soft glow of the fire, the Mayan could see the Lakota scoff while shaking her head. She muttered impatiently under her breath then left back out the door.

At her departure, the Mayan sighed a breath of relief... content with herself that she had so cleverly fooled the Lakota woman.

There was activities within the camp long before the sun rose. Tall-Eagle wanted to clear out at the sun's first light. So in the cold gray of dawn, his people were deconstructing their sleeping lodges and making them ready for the travois. The stark black of night gradually turn to subtle shades of gray... shades of gray that was slowly giving way to pinkish and purple hues as the sun's light reached up into the heavens... banishing the darkness. The moon had slipped beyond the distant hills. Still, the Morning-Star dominated the heaven.

Tall-Eagle lent help where it was needed. In expert fashion, the entire camp was quickly being dismantled. White-Sun and Mocking-Bird was cooking for the band. He didn't like the fact that the fire was out in the open... flames sputtering and crackling in the dim brightness of an icy-spring dawn. He felt it left the two women exposed to the Crow. He paused for a moment to gaze intensely about the sweeping prairie. To the east, beyond the purple fringes of the fading darkness, he saw movement upon a distant hill. He knew it was the Crow.

He went to urge his band to hasten their pace but caught a glimpse of the Mayan as she emerged from a tipi, her wild hair and soft features capturing his complete attention. He watched as she slowly rose to her feet... looking about the camp as if seeking something... or searching for someone.

Upon seeing the Deer-Lady emerging from the lodge of White-Sun, three scouts immediately went to work taking it apart.

"Are you ready for the day's journey?" Tall-Eagle asked the Deer-Lady.

"I am," she said simply.

"Get enough to eat?"

"I did."

"Well-rested?"

"I am."

"This is good," Tall-Eagle said. He then looked about the camp. The horses were being loaded, soon they would depart. Under normal circumstances, the Little-Star-Band possessed magnificent horses. They were swift... strong... and sure-footed. They were of a gentle nature... retained no signs of being mean spirited. But under the current pressure, they look strained and wary. This bothered Tall-Eagle.

Turns-Black brought Tall-Eagle the horse that had been left behind for him. The steed wasn't like his beloved Strong-Spirit... but it was easily gaited and gentle in nature... which was good enough for him.

The horse made his way towards the Deer-Lady. And let out a soft neigh while bobbing its massive head up and down. The Mayan naturally reach up to pet its mane. The horse tenderly nuzzled her shoulder and neck.

"It seems as if this horse is quite fond of you," Tall-Eagle said as he reached up a hand to rub between the horse's eyes. "He really likes you."

"Perhaps," the Mayan simply replied.

"Perhaps this horse is wiser than a Crow." After saying this he gazed upon the Mayan. He smiled first with his eyes... and then with his lips.

It was the first time the Mayan had truly noticed his smile. Despite being a warrior, he had a nice smile. A smile that was easy and unforced. A smile that had a way of putting her at ease.

She was about to respond with her own smile when she noticed Left-Wing approaching.

"So you can speak?" he asked in Lakota with a disgusting snare. "And could you not have spoken when I had asked?" he drew closer as he questioned her, dwarfing the tall Mayan immediately.

"She doesn't speak Lakota," Tall-Eagle answered when he realized how abruptly her face had darkened.

The Deer-Lady felt transfixed by the fear-mongers terrible gaze. Every time he spoke to her, he spoke with such arrogance... such mockery. Within... she could feel fear slithering through her... like a boa... constricting her heart and chest.

She looked past Left-Wing at Tall-Eagle... the dark pools of her eyes soft brown eyes swirling with emotions. But above all... her eyes were filled with desperate hope.

"Now is not the time, Left-Wing. She has been through a lot," Tall-Eagle said Lakota, the expression he shot at Left-Wing said more forcefully than his words could have.

Left-Wing feigned a look of surprise as he grinned a wolfish grin that had a kind of ruthless charm to it. "I wish only to speak to the one that had led us to war."

"Principle had let us to war. Standing for what is right had led us to war. Not her." His words, swift as an arrow, had caught Left-Wing by surprise.

"Again you speak what is true," Left-Wing had said, once again by way of apology.

Checking his tone, Tall-Eagle said, "She speaks Hopi."

"What is your name?" he asked the Mayan in the Hopi language.

Trying her very best to ignore the uneasiness that continued to slither through her, she answered, "I am aware that I am called the Deer-Lady," it was only with great effort was she able to keep her voice firm and secure.

But the well-honed eyes of Left-Wing saw that he had her startled... and he seemed rather grimly delighted in this knowledge. "Before, when I asked if you spoke Hopi, why did you not answer me then?" he asked. He didn't possess an accusatory tone within his question... but there seems to be a kind of laughter just beneath the surface of the question.

The Mayan didn't respond. Instead... she looked up at Tall-Eagle... her eyes reaching out to him. Left-Wing felt something twist deep within his own heart. She looked so vulnerable... so lost and alone. "Now I see why you wish to keep her," he said to Tall-Eagle in Lakota.

"There is much to be done," Tall-Eagle said to Left-Wing.

"We are done. We are ready for the journey," Left-Wing retorted.

"There is much to be done," Tall-Eagle repeated... there was a twinge of annoyance within his tone.

Left-Wing lifted his head towards the heavens and raised his palms in an exaggerated manner. With a false quiver in his voice, he asks a Great-Spirit, "Why must my oldest friend be so cruel?" He then turned and stomped off.

The Mayan felt relieved to see him go. She knew not what he said... but his mannerisms were enough to border on the offensive. "It seems," she said to Tall-Eagle, "everything he utters has to be done in a slightly bemused and mocking tone."

"He is a fine warrior. And it's heart is good. Sometimes, he knows not when to be serious."

The grassy hills twinkled and sparkled with dew in the bright morning sun. Red-River observed the Lakota from a distant hill. He observed as the band dismantled their lodges at an impressive speed. The first laden travois with wary ponies had set out before the first rays of the sun caressed the land.

He wanted so desperately to claim his prize. But he knew his Crow warriors were still outnumbered. He knew he had to bide his time... for soon the enemies of his enemy would arrive. And then he will claim what is rightfully his.

The Little-Star-Band had broken camp before the morning sun had risen. Left-Wing and Pretty-Elk rode ahead as the vanguard. Tall-Eagle, along with the Mayan, took up the rear. He wanted to keep a watchful eye on the Crow. But from this position, he led his people over the tall prairie grass... leading them towards the edge of the plains... leading them towards the land of the Oglala.

The band was silent as their horses strained against the burden of their travois. Their footfalls were upon a wet earth... the heavy cold dampening all sounds so that the passing was barely audible.

The sun was at its highest point in the sky before Tall-Eagle broke the silence. By then the morning dew had long ago evaporated and a warm gentle breeze caused the tall grass to sway peacefully.

"Look," Tall-Eagle said softly.

The Mayan followed his gaze and found two curious coyotes on the nearby hill; they're gray coats blending in perfectly with the shadows. The pair watched as the band pressed solemnly onward. They then trotted it to the next hill, and there they sat, watching the intruders.

Tall-Eagle was thankful for the coyotes, for now, he had reason to speak without appearing anxious. "They will continue to follow us until we leave their territory."

But the Mayan didn't respond, for her mind was trying to wrap itself around her current situation. Although she couldn't see them, she knew the Crow were following them. Deep within, she could feel the chill of their intent... the searing coldness of their determination. She knew she wasn't at Lakota prisoner... but still, she felt trapped. She couldn't leave. Perhaps this was what the Crow were waiting for? She had no choice but to trust this Tall-Eagle. Against her most basic, most primal instinct, she trusted him. She didn't know why. The long and hard years had taught her the basic truth of man. The blood of her people, the blood of 8 million Mayans bore painful witness to this reality... this basic truth. But again... where could she go?

Tall-Eagle was peripherally aware that the Mayan was staring down at him. Inwardly, a gleam of hope had come to him. Even so... he continued to stare about the Great-Plains... catching brief glimpses of the gray coyotes in the bright light of the sun. Then they would disappear within shadows again.

"Tell me about your people," the Mayan whispered.

Throughout the day they travel and talked. He could tell by her body language that she was considerably more relaxed. When he asked about her pierced ears, she said all Mayan women have pierced earlobes. They would wear earrings made of jade or gold to enhance their beauty. Tall-Eagle had to resist an overwhelming urge to tell the Mayan how beautiful she was... even without earrings. He was unfamiliar with the jade or gold, he had come to learn what they were. This yellow rock that the pale-faces crave, this yellow rock that made them crazy and dangerous... this was gold.

Before long the conversation became personal. Each knew they were treading upon sacred ground... so the other would sit quietly as the other told their story.

Twilight descending upon them as lengthening and deepening shadows stretched across the prairie. Again Brave-Shield and Blue-Leaf were sent out ahead to find a suitable location for the band to make their camp.

They found a small patch of woods nestled inside a shadowy valley.

Darkness had soon blotted out the formation of tree trunks. Tall-Eagle thought it was wise that no fires were to be made. Instead, they ate the remaining dried berry-cakes, along with jerk-venison and buffalo strips. In the light of a half-moon, he could see the toll this journey was taken upon his People. And their insatiable appetites further attested to the strenuous few days that have had.

Quick lean-tos were erected and people were already falling asleep. Tall-Eagle appointed a total of eight warriors to stand guard instead of the usual four. He did this because as he looked about, these moving shadows provided a natural cover for attacks. Again he took the first watch. He sat with his back posted against the trunk of a tree... his well-trained eyes never wavering in their constant surveying of his surroundings. The heavy smell of decaying wood and budding leaves was a strange but pleasant mixture to him. And there he sat... listening as a bird chirp it's good night song to anyone who cared to listen.

That night, the Mayan slept upon an earth made warm by plush buffalo robes. She lay beneath whispering pines with White-Sun and Mocking-Bird. She had eaten her fill... and it wasn't long before slept crept upon her. Before she submitted to the realm of sleep, she thought of Tall-Eagle and their many conversations throughout the day. He was the last thought she had. For the first time in many, many years, that night no evil spirits came to mar her dreams... for it was the first time she didn't fear that something or someone would come to harm her.

The Mayan was awakened by the cheerful song of a mocking-bird. Looking around she found that she was alone. Stepping from beneath the coziness of pines, she saw that morning within the woods came with a color mixture that intensified the spirit. Despite the morning chill... everything was warm and welcoming. More birds were singing as squirrels ran about the tree branches... yelling in their tiny voices at the intruders.

The Little-Star-Band had already retrieved their horses and we're loading them.

"Blankets," White-Sun said to the Deer-Lady. "Bring them," she said as she motioned with her hand. The Mayan understood the gesture and did as instructed. Her buffalo robes were the last to be loaded upon the pony-drags.

One by one they exited the wooded area. Before them, they witnessed beautiful grassy hills that glittered in the bright morning sun. To the left, the endless sweep of a valley opened up before them. Parts of it untouched by the golden fingers of sunlight that's so eloquently caressed the rest of the valley. From there, The Little-Star-Band continued to follow the faithful path of the sun, both them and the sun making their way towards the west.

The band followed the same pattern as the day before with Left-Wing and Pretty-Elk in front, while Tall-Eagle and the Deer-Lady brought up the rear. The Mayan rode while the Lakota walked. Tall-Eagle had yet to see another Crow. But he knew they were there... watching... waiting.

At midday the band came upon a sparkling stream. By this time the Mayan had become quite comfortable with her new surroundings. She leapt from her horse and led it to the stream beside Left-Wing. Her horse's coat was glistening with perspiration... the poor creature looked so weary.

She used her hand as a cup, dribbling the freshwater upon the horse's fur. She patted its glossy neck and gave it a small hug. The creature understood the affection given to it by the Mayan. It sat patiently as it was being washed... every so often it would nibble upon the Mayans sleeve.

This caused the Mayan to chuckle to herself.

Tall-Eagle stood watching the love that was being shown to the horse. And hearing the Mayan laugh had touched him so deeply... so profound... he knew at that very moment that he would give his life to protect the innocence of this woman... this Deer-Lady... this Mayan.

Realizing she was being observed, the Mayan fell into a deep silence. As she continued to wash the horse she would steal glances at the acting chief.

"Notice you are the only one washing your horse," he said as he approached.

She looked at the other horses. Their burdens were set aside as they were given an opportunity to rest. The Lakota people were either bathing in the stream, eating, or preparing a small fire to purify drinking water. The horses stood beside and eddy. Here they drink and gazed on the tall grass that hung over the flowing waters. She watched as the horses kicked and bit at one another. She then refocused the attention upon her own horse... a horse that seemed to be looking at her. As she stared into the blank lenses of her horse... she saw a ghostly reflection of herself.

"These horses carry the burden of your people," she said to Tall-Eagle as she continued to stroke the horse's neck. "The spirit of this horse allows me to sit upon his back. I am its burden. But he accepts me. And for this I am grateful." As she said this she looked over her shoulder at Tall-Eagle. She was surprised at what she saw.

Tall-Eagle was frowning as he stared across the stream... an intense expression of preoccupation plastered on his face. She followed his gaze and found a lone warrior standing on the distant bank. The horse he sat upon seem to be nervous... as if it knew that war was sure to follow.

Left-Wing and Big-Scout rushed to the side of Tall-Eagle, their horses too sensing a sort of danger.

Almost immediately two dozen new warriors appeared along the hill just beyond the bank.

Even from that distance, Tall-Eagle could see by their clothes and feathers that they were the warriors of the Ponca Tribe. They were former enemies of the Lakota. But they had not been in open war with each other for many, many winters.

Big-Scout leapt from his horse and gave it to the acting chief. In a fluid motion, Tall-Eagle was upon the great beast.

He's tapped the pony with a heel of his moccasins and he and Left-Wing begin to cross the stream... their horses splashing water everywhere as their yelps urge them forward.

The Mayan watch as Tall-Eagle and Left-Wing made it to the other side. The group of warriors moved together as a single unit down the hill. They disappeared as they near the bottom but soon reappeared just beyond the bank of the stream. Their high cheek-bone faces were painted impressively, the Mayan noticed. The aura they emitted seemed supremely confident and deadly.

She noticed that all the young horse watchers had gathered all the ponies. They were pulling them together near her. She saw their faces. These young scouts tried to hide their fears... keeping their young faces silent and blank. But she read the truth in their eyes.

A cold chill pass through the soul of the Deer-Lady.

"They are the Quapaw from the Ponca Tribe," Pretty-Elk said to the Mayan in the Hopi language. "They are proud and willful. They were once our enemy. A truce was agreed upon many winters ago," he said. "But I wonder what they are doing this for North?" he said silently to himself.

"I read fear in the eyes of the young ones," the Mayan said, barely above a whisper. She knew very few of the Lakota could speak Hopi. Only those that had traveled for trading purposes could understand the conversation, for they were too young to have been in Tribal Council. Even so, she didn't want to offend anyone.

"There is just cause for this," Pretty-Elk said as he stepped closer to the Deer-Lady. "Something is amiss, for in other times they would have greeted us with kind words. With food and drink, for they are generous and thoughtful in deed. But now, they stand silent... dressed as if prepared for war."

"Will they attack?" whispered the Deer-Lady

"They are true-hearted and will not break their word. But like our young scouts, I too feel a strange twinge of expectancy. As if something dark and menacing is approaching."

Pretty-Elk and the Mayan fell into a heavy silence... quietly observing the Lakota warriors standing proudly before the many Ponca warriors.

Unconsciously... her mind began to wander into dangerous and unpleasant territories. Bitter memories flashed before her mind's eye. As a child... she remembered watching her father approach the Spanish conquistadors in peace.

Her father... strong and proud... standing before those who weld spears of fire and destruction. Standing before them in a humble way... open and exposed. Exposed in a way a wolf would display it's soft underside to the alpha male. This is exactly what her father did... lay before the Spanish with the most vulnerable flesh of his neck and belly exposed... praying against prayer his soft flesh would not be devoured.

Such prayers were to no avail... for the Mayan god of wanton destruction had a hunger for flesh on that day.

The Spanish, who weld spears of fire and destruction, had raised their weapons to the heavens. Thunder boom as lightning spat from the tips of their spears. And from this lightning buzzed invisible, but angry hornets that seemed to rip and devour the flesh of her father. The force of these carnivorous hornets had blew her father backward... as if kicked in his chest by an invisible god. Blood... as fine as mist, seemed to hover above her father.

All at once... the world grew silent.

Metal swords were drawn as horses reared up on their hind legs. The men and women of her village began to scream as they dove for cover.

Fires were set to their dwellings. Wild dogs were set loose upon the villagers. The entire city was consumed by blazing fires that distorted the sounds. She saw women and children running... their mouths gaping in silent screams.

She knew they were screaming, but she could not hear them. She could hear nothing... nothing but the deep erratic breathing and the beating of her own heart. A heart that seemed to pound directly on her eardrums.

She took a step towards her father. He laid there... withering in torturous pain. His fingers probing questioningly at the torn flesh of his chest.

Slowly she fell to her knees... her tiny hands clasping her father's blood-soaked hands. He tried to look at his daughter... but his pain-filled eyes were unable to focus.

With trembling fingers, she tried applying pressure. The blood of her father felt hot and thick as a seeped for beneath tiny hands.

All around her, her people were being slaughtered. Swords and muskets were laying waste to everything she had ever known... laying waste to everything she had ever loved. And then the darkness came. Everything went blank.

She was on her knees when the conquistador rode upon her. With her back to him, he planted the stock of his weapon into the back of her head. The powerful blow reverberated up his arms and threw his shoulders. He felt and heard something give way under the blow. He falsely believed that the child's skull fractured under his heavy weapon, when in fact it was the wooden stock that has splintered at the point of impact.

The little girl slumped over her father... her warm blood mixing with his. With the last of his energy he cradled his daughter's head. With his last breath, he prayed his daughter would survive. Then the life and pain drain from his tattered body.

The little girl was awakened by a sharp pain. The pain of her flesh being ripped from her face.

The sun had long fallen below the western skies. A full moon in the cloud-filled skies cast about a gray and eerie hue. Thick, gray clouds, like gray brains, floating upon a velvet black sky made the carnage seem surreal.

Again, the feeling of her flesh being ripped from her face returned. In pain, she cried out. A cry that startled the vulture that tried feeding upon the unconscious child. The great scavenger squawked and opened its mighty wings as it danced backward.

The little girl tried to sit up, but found her head was being held in a cold embrace. The putrid stench of blood that lingered in the air was so powerful that it made her stomach tighten. She wished she could stop breathing it.

Again she tried to sit up, but couldn't. To her horror, she realized she was being held by her father. Rigor mortis had set in and the warmth of his flesh had fled long ago. His cold embrace prevented her from moving.

The vulture had returned, slipping its smooth head and neck through his cold arms... seeking the warm and soft flesh of her face.

Again she screamed and again the scavenger let out his own screech while hopping backward... its great wings fluttering wildly.

With all the strength she could gather, she pulled herself from her father's grasp. Her head throbbed with the beat of her racing heart. All around her was death and feeding vultures. In the gray light of the moon, she watched in horror as those vultures rip at the dead flesh with grim alacrity... tearing and packing... then tossing its bloody head back so that the unholy repast can fall down their slender throats.

She turned to her father... only to find his eyes have been plucked from their sockets. His gaping mouth seemed to cry out in silent rage.

The vulture returned. But instead of going towards her, it hopped towards her father's head. Before she could react, it slipped its grayish pink head into her father's mouth and halfway down his throat.

A piercing scream had snapped the Mayan from her terrifying vision. She tried looking around, trying to find the source of the screen. But nothing seemed real. Before her stood Pretty-Elk. He took ahold of her shoulders and was speaking to her. But his words seemed to echo in the feverish haze that felt like a dream.

He shook her once. Then twice. In a moment... the Mayan... so full of pain and dismay... became aware that the screaming was emanating from her very own lips.

Slowly, her eyes refocused. Again she found herself with the Lakota People, standing beside a sparkling stream that sang a beautiful song. The bright sun stood high and proud in the afternoon skies. The morning chill had been replaced by a warm, gentle breeze. A breeze that caused the prairie grass to bellow and ripple in cascading waves like an endless sea... swaying and washing until it met the heavens far off in the distance.

Across the stream, she saw both Tall-Eagle and Left-Wing staring in her direction. But their attention quickly went back to the Ponca warriors that stood before them.

"Are you okay?" Pretty-Elk asked the Mayan.

Slowly she ran her eyes about herself. The entire Little-Star-Band was staring at her. Brave-Shield was trying to soothe the startled horse that she had bathed. The weary beast was pulling against the reins in fear.

"I am fine," she said in a weak and shallow voice. "I fear for Tall-Eagle," she said as she, herself, hid from the truth. A truth she had tried so hard to repress. A truth she never wanted to face. She lifted a hand to her cheek to feel the old wound. The vulture had left an everlasting mark on the Mayan... both mentally and physically. The scar had healed over and faded with time. Even so, under the right lights it is visible.

Pretty-Elk could only stare in helplessly. He felt a surge of pity for her fire through him. Something was truly amiss with his Mayan stranger. But it would have to wait.

The two Lakota emissaries return shortly. Tall-Eagle's eyes held an air of concern, while Left-Wing eyes were lit with the fires of battle. "We must depart, quickly," Tall-Eagle said to Pretty-Elk in Lakota. His tone suggested the band should move with haste.

"The Crow had been through," Left-Wing said to Pretty-Elk. "They tried to recruit our former enemies. The Ponca had informed the Crow that no conflict existed between them and us directly. Even so, almost half of the Ponca elders wanted to join our enemies against us," Left-Wing spat as if ingesting something distasteful.

A mask of disbelief came over the face of Pretty-Elk.

"By way of vote they opted not to take sides," Tall-Eagle said sternly. There was a hint of desperation lurking in his voice... a kind of rage at the life his people now lead... and the cruelty of it all.

"Yet, they dress as if prepare for war?" Left-Wing question as he became livid with anger. "Why not appease the Ponca Elders who wish to go to war with us? I vote we cross this stream and put it into these two-faced cowards and their story."

"My young friend speaks in anger," Tall-Eagle said to Pretty-Elk. "Which is why we never leave such decisions to the rash of youth. They are prepared to defend themselves against the Crow were they to retaliate for rejecting their offer. Lakota are not the reason they are dressed for war."

Pretty-Elk said nothing... he simply nodded his head in slow agreement. In frustration, Left-Wing kicked his horse and begin rounding up the People of the Little-Star-Band... preparing them to ride out as quickly as possible.

In that moment of silence, Tall-Eagle locked eyes with Pretty-Elk. With a slight tilt of his head, he inquired about the Mayan and her scream. A flicker of sadness crept into his eyes as he barely shook his head at the acting chief.

Tall-Eagle turned his inquisitive gaze towards the Deer-Lady. She stood silently, staring at the ground, her posture radiating embarrassment. But still, she stood tall and proud. And above all... beautiful. So beautiful. There was something about this Mayan that suggested an almost inexhaustible power of resilience.

The Little-Star-Band were on the move once again. The Ponca had escorted the band from a safe distance... following as the Lakota made it to the edge of their territory. Both Tall-Eagle and Left-Wing knew they were being shadowed. This caused great hostility to form in the depths of Left-Wing's heart.

"Are we to run until we can run no more?" Left-Wing asked Tall-Eagle.

"You will get your war, my young friend," the acting chief whispered cryptically. "Soon you will get your war," he repeated, barely above a whisper.

But such assurance did little to comfort the anxious warrior.

In silence they travel, over an ocean of green earth... undulated in heavy, long-drawn waves that pressed on and on into the blue distance. The Lakota People walked in pairs. The body of No-Horns laid wrap tightly in the center of the line. Twice that day they had to switch the pony that dragged the young fallen warrior. They were all weary... drained... tired.

It was the reasoning of Pretty-Elk that finally broke the heavy pall of silence. "How did the Ponca surprise us? Are we that weary?" he asked as he approached Tall-Eagle and the Deer-Lady. "Perhaps the journey is taking its toll upon our scouts?" he said cautiously, but with a steady note of genuine concern lining his voice. He didn't want to overstep his bounds. It was the acting chief's ultimate decision.

Tall-Eagle knew his words were true... his people and their ponies were in desperate need of rest.

Again two scouts were sent forth to find a suitable camping ground.

The sun... a disc of golden fire, had tipped the bleak horizon when they finally made it to the temporal home. The site was upon a great bluff that rendered a beautiful panoramic view. He felt reassurance that no intruder could approach without being spotted. The setting sun had set the surrounding hills on fire with scarlet and gold colors.

The acting chief slowly and deeply inhaled through his nose... taking in the fresh scents of Mother-Earth. Then slowly release the pent-up breath through barely parted lips. "This is good," he said quietly as he slowly nodded his head. For the first time in many days... he felt his people were safe and secure. "This is good," he repeated as he looked upon Left-Wing and White-Sun. "Tonight we feast, then rest well." And like that, the Little-Star-Band quickly erected the lodges and set fires to prepare the meals.

Red-River and a selected few stayed a safe distance from the Lakota. He was sure that the Lakota knew they were being followed. Even so... he wanted to torture the imaginations of his enemy.

He traveled only with a few. The bulk of his warriors were even further behind. Just in case they were spotted, he didn't want the Sioux to know the true numbers of his ever-expanding forces. When the time to attack finally came... he wanted the onslaught to be a complete surprise.

Dark anticipation filled him as he thought about the prize he was sure to inherit... Bull's-Tail. At the thought he felt his lips pulled into a grimace of a grin.

"It seems they are stopping for the night," Black-Feather said, interrupting his thoughts.

"Then send word to the main group," Red-River fumes angrily. Black-Feather held Red-River's angry gaze for an insolent moment... his own eyes smoldering with great hostility. But he turned away and stalked off in the direction of the main group.

Red-River then returned his focus to the distant bluff. Upon its crown he could see the Lakota erecting tipis and building fires. No doubt the Ponca had warned the Sioux that the Crow had already been through here, recruiting warriors. They may have been unsuccessful with the Ponca... but how foolish the Lakota must be to assume all their attempts have been unsuccessful.

A sinister thought had bounced into his mind at that moment. A thought designed to further torture the Lakota. He decided... the next morning he will appear before the Lakota. In full war regalia, he will stalk their camp. He will be alone... but in the anxious minds of his enemies, they will assume the time for open war had finally come.

Again he felt his lips tug into a tight smile.

Tall-Eagle sat alone inside his lodge. The sweet smell of cedar and sage smoke lingered in the quiet space. All about the camp, its inhabitants went about their own routine. Their eyes constantly shifting towards the outer perimeter... a byproduct of the days darkened by the threats of all-out war.

At that very moment, the Deer-Lady was going from lodge to lodge. With her, she carried a bag of water... offering a drink to all. He searched his mind for reasons to talk to her when she came. Above his sleeping area... Tall-Eagle had a small black and white beaded dreamcatcher. A dreamcatcher that was decorated with feathers belonging to a golden eagle dangling from it. To him it was sacred... and he took it with him wherever he went. But he had seen her staring at it... perhaps she was as captivated by its beauty as he was. This seemed to be the perfect excuse.

The Deer-Lady stopped in front of his lodge... holding out the bag of water as an offering. Behind her... the scene was bathed in an eerie glow of the dawn of a new day. An eerie glow illuminated her profile from behind as she stood in front of him. The dawn's light was trapped in her hair... creating a faint halo of golden brown light that radiated from her head in luminous beauty.

"Would you like some water?" she asked in that voice that was just the side of husky. Her narrow face retained her mask of seriousness. But despite the perpetual expression of solemnity... she would often demonstrate an expression of warmth and kindness.

"I have something to show you," Tall-Eagle said to the Deer-Lady.

Tall-Eagle reached for the medicine bundle he kept at the foot of his sleeping area. This spiritual bundle was wrapped in red leather. Red... the rainbow color for protection. Red... the color of blood... the color of life... the color of ritual.

Slowly and delicately he untied the red leather straps and carefully unrolled the bundle. Inside laid an eagle's wing... a ceremonial fan that had a beaded handle. There were also lose feathers belonging to a golden eagle. And from these loose feathers, he pulled out one he found truly unique and held it to where the Deer-Lady could see.

"Have you ever witness such a strange feather?" he asked.

The golden eagle feather was the length of a man's forearm. It's black body with gray stripes, with a faint white that look like thick rolling smoke. The golden eagle feather had always been prized among the Lakota woman for its beauty. But this is the first feather he had ever seen with a white tip. Tall-Eagle had grown up around feathers... and has seen as many feathers as there are stars in the heavens. But never had he seen one with a white tip.

"Have you ever seen such a feather?" he repeated. The Deer-Lady's eyes went to the feather... but Tall-Eagle was unable to read her expression. "Have you ever seen one with a white tip?"

After a moment of observing the feather, she asked, "Is that an owl feather?"

Tall-Eagle had to remind himself that this woman was from the far south and would be unfamiliar with feathers... for feathers held no importance in her culture.

"It's from a golden eagle," he said as he held it up to her. Despite the cultural differences... she knew she couldn't touch it... for it was considered sacred to the Lakota people. But Tall-Eagle wanted so desperately to give it to her... as a gift... as a token. But the rules and traditions of the People forbade it.

"Does the white tip mean its bad luck?" she acquired as her interest grew.

"We don't believe in luck. Good or otherwise. We believe only in truth... divine and natural. "

"You don't believe in luck?" she asked as she began to relax in his presence. "Don't you believe if you see an owl is bad luck?" The Deer-Lady inquired.

"Why do you ask that?" Tall-Eagle implored.

"I was told so. Many winters ago one of my relatives fell ill. And I saw an owl... and within weeks... he went to the Land-of-the-Spirits."

"Because of the owl?" he asked almost mockingly, and instantly regretting it.

For several moments an uneasy silence enveloped the two... like an insulting cocoon. Tall-Eagle didn't mean to inject a mocking tone into his voice. But before the moment was ruined, he continued... "For our enemies, the owl may be considered a bird of ill fate. For it's the creature of the night we mimic when coordinating or attack."

The woman looked at him confusingly... not fully understanding his meaning.

"In darkness it is hard to see," Tall-Eagle stated. "And in this darkness we try to surround our enemies. In order for us to remain hidden, we cannot use our voices to say where we are. So we mimic the creatures of the night. The owl is especially useful when communicating with our brothers of war."

As he spoke he gestured with his hands. And then he cuffed them over his mouth and let out a soft hoot.

The Deer-Lady gave one of her rare smiles when he mimicked the sound of an owl taking flight... that heartbreakingly beautiful smile of hers that reveals her dimples. A sudden breeze caught her brown curly hair... whipping it across her face... she made no attempt to pull it back.

And there... for a brief moment... their eyes locked. Her liquid brown eyes... soft and trusting... staring into the dark eyes of the warrior. Eyes that spoke of a life of bitter conflicts. But in that small... tiny moment... the warrior had encountered the very essence of the Dear-Lady's spirit... and his own spirit flickered in its power. Despite himself... Tall-Eagle gave a genuine smile... and his face turned boyish.

"Well I grew up Catholic," the Deer-Lady finally said... shattering what Tall-Eagle thought was a moment of two kindred souls combining. "Catholic is the religion of the conquerors of the South," she explained further.

"So do you believe in luck?"

"There may be some truth to it," she replied in the low, unconvincing tone. "The world is a strange place... is it not?"

Tall-Eagle slowly nodded his head as he carefully began to fold his feather in the red leather carrying case. With a small smile still playing along his lip, he looked back up at the Deer-Lady.

"I can feel them," the Deer-Lady said as her tone became solemn. She spoke in a voice a little more than a soft whisper... but her eyes were wide with fright. "They are here. Watching."

"Who?" Tall-Eagle asked as he rose to his feet.

"Enemies of the Lakota," she said cryptically. "Enemies of Peace."

Tall-Eagle looked to his weapons. There were two different bows in his lodge... one for the hunt... the chase. And the second for combat.

The warrior grabbed his bow for war and quiver and brushed passed a Deer-Lady. Once outside he turned his gaze towards the east... where the rising sun was painting a beautiful golden nimbus at the horizon... the clouds were thinly torn and drifting slowly. The skyline was clear.

He knew they were being followed by Crow scouts... no doubt relaying their every movement to their counterparts. But these scouts had remained craftily hidden. The Lakota scouts hadn't seen so much as an enemy feather... let alone an enemy warrior along the skyline.

Tall-Eagle turned back towards the Deer-Lady... who now surveyed the eastern hills herself. She then looked at Tall-Eagle... her brown eyes were wide and troubled... searching his eyes for much needed reassurance. "They are closer. Of this I am sure."

Tall-Eagle felt a surge of pity for her. The imagined horrors of being forced into a miserable life of servitude amongst a savage people in a foreign land. He wanted desperately to reach out to her... to comfort her. But he respectfully kept his distance.

At that moment, the early morning silence was shattered by a war cry.

Tall-Eagle looked off into the distance and spotted a loan warrior upon a horse... a horse who danced along the skyline of a distant hill. Instantly he knew it was the Crow warrior, Red-River. Upon his crown he had a bristled mohawk and a face painted red and black.

Red river set upon his anxious horse in the early cold... glaring at the campsite with open speculation. Tall-Eagle watched as he drew even closer.

Alerted by the Lakota scouts... men were bursting from their tipis with weapons in hand... calling out to each other in excitement and bloodlust.

Left-wing appeared at the edge of the camp... his face ablaze with excitement... his bow in hand... trying to bring it up to bear.

"Wait!" Tall-Eagle called out to the young warrior.

Confuse, Left-Wing lowered his weapon and looked back at the acting chief. But Tall-Eagle said nothing more.

A strange... ominous silence has settled over the campsite... for every eye was fixed upon the loan warrior. And behind each pair of those dark eyes flared resentment.

Turning away from Tall-Eagle, Left-Wing went to raise his bow again... aiming directly towards the intruder.

"Wait!" Tall-Eagle demanded sharply... and then started walking towards him. Again, Left-Wing lowered his bow and looked confusingly at Tall-Eagle.

Only the sounds of the restless Lakota horses could be heard... as they whined and neighed, plumes of gray fog flared from the wide and open nostrils.

"My arrow grows restless in my hands," Left-Wing said to Tall-Eagle as he held an arrow loosely by its shaft... but it remained unstrung.

"If you fire now then you will fire too soon," Tall-Eagle told the anxious warrior. "His pride and arrogance would draw him within range. We cannot let him know how powerful your bow is."

Red-River continued to slowly move towards the campsite... his war paint twisting his features in feral resentment... foolish pride and jealous anger conquering him. Believing he was still out of range of the deadly arrows... he continued to move closer.

Left-Wing's bow was carved from hickory... double-strung with thick sinew. He was the greatest hunter within all the tribes for two reasons... his ability to seemingly walk on air... and the distance is arrow will fly from the finely crafted bow.

Red-River stopped at the bottom of the hill... his horse still bobbing his head and stomping it's hooves. He raised his lance and let out a mighty bellow. "Open war lies before you!" he warned.

Red-River continued to move closer.

Tall-Eagle gave Left-Wing the signal to fire. Left-Wing's face flared with fiery excitement as he raised bow and drew the string. The sinew thong pulled smoothly past his lips and cheek... ending slightly past his ear. Tall-Eagle listen to the power of the bow in it's almost silent bending. He then released the heavy tension... sending the daily projectile sailing through the air towards the unexpecting Crow enemy.

Although Tall-Eagle hadn't seen where the arrow had landed... it had to have fallen dangerously close... for with astonishing skill and speed, the Crow warrior wheeled his horse and retreated back up the hill... stopping only once he reached the top. Again he turned around... raising his lance in a defiant gesture... roaring again with all his primeval fury.

Left-Wing turned to Tall-Eagle with a sly, mischievous grin... which caused the other warriors amongst them to chuckle with a sense of relaxation. Even Tall-Eagle himself couldn't help but laugh... for without ever witnessing the awesome strength of Left-Wing's bow... one would never believe the distance his arrow could cover.

The acting chief then looked at the Deer-Lady. The relaxed laughter seemed to armor her against and eroding doubts... and then... the torrid blood of her diverged ancestry converted the fear and doubt into a smoldering anger that flared in her brown eyes. Her thin lips protruded even further... creating a thin line of hatred... making her look even more deer-like.

This caused Tall-Eagle to laugh a second time. But her hot eyes never left the distant hill... where the intruder stayed precariously perched atop of a dancing horse.

"Let us break camp," Tall-Eagle said gently... not wanting to spoil the mood of his People. Then he slowly and painfully realized this was the first in many suns where his people were genuinely relaxed.

Oh, how he longed to see the People of Oglala... for with them there will be a true sense of safety for his People... for they were dependable allies. And again they could laugh and smile... and perhaps... dream once again of love.

Pretty-Elk and Big-Nose gathered their wary ponies... half of which were on the verge of becoming lame from the harsh and brutal flight. The makeshift council decided to lighten their burden by leaving behind all nonessentials. A few of the warriors even volunteered to leave their tipis behind and opt to use a lean-to instead. And before their departure they created a bonfire... where they burned everything they choose to leave behind. They didn't want their personal items to be spoils of war for the ensuing Crow.

The hissing fire wildly flickered as bellows of black smoke reached for the heavens. It seemed to rise up and darkening the morning sun... turning it the hue of blood. The flames danced feverishly as it ate away at the furs and hides of elks and buffaloes. Tall-Eagle watched in silence... ensuring nothing usable survived the flames.

The heat of the fire touched his flesh... warming him... chasing away the night's cold. He had ordered his people not to wear leggings despite the morning chill. It was still cold... but soon they would be warm for the coolness of dawn would soon dissipate into the muggy dry heat of the plains. And he did not want to have to slow down as people changed. Besides... the heat of their bodies will rise as they move.

Morning had broken over the plains when they finally departed... pouring a flood of light glazing over the land. Stretched before them was an open sea as far as the eye could see. A sea of nothing but gentle rolling hills of swaying grass. Grass that was green in the spring... golden in the summer.

As they traversed the grassy sea they did so under the watchful eye of Red-River. There upon the crest of a hill he sat... Tall-Eagle knew beyond a shadow of a doubt that there were more warriors on the other side of the hill... but their numbers aren't strong enough to yet launch an attack. This is why they remain hidden. But if the threats of Red-River were true... then assume their numbers will grow... for history shows that the Lakota made enemies all too easy.

At one point Tall-Eagle saw a second Crow warrior riding beside Red-River. He then raced ahead towards the Lakota people. Only to stop short... circled his horse twice... then kicked it into a full gallop... disappearing to the far side of the hill.

"After the night attack two days ago the Crow felt there is no need to hide," Tall-Eagle said to the Deer-Lady as she drew near. He saw that she kept throwing nervous glances over her shoulders. "They know that we are aware of their presence. But we don't know the size of their force. This is why they keep at a distance."

The Deer-Lady said nothing as they followed a struggling pony...

his step faltering under the weights of the travois. Tall-Eagle knew it would be easy for anybody to track this party. For the thick lines of parted grass could be easily seen at a distance... the deep trenches left by the dragging travois couldn't be easily covered even if one were to try.

Let them follow, Tall-Eagle thought to himself... soon we will be in the land of the Oglala.

The hot sun was directly overhead when one of his scouts came riding towards the party. He stopped his pony just before Tall-Eagle and the Deer-Lady. Tall-Eagle instantly recognized the burning mix of rage and sadness in the depths of the young scout's eyes. The scout said nothing... but the expression said more than words ever could.

The Deer-Lady could feel the hurt and pain and the burning desire for vengeance radiating from the young scout. A desire so powerful she has to force herself to close her senses to the song of his hatred that sprang from his heart.

Somberly, Tall-Eagle looked over to her... reaching out to her with wide eyes. He would often open himself up to her freely through his eyes. And there she would catch a glimpse into the secrets of his heart. But as always... she forced herself to look away.

The scout returned leading a second pony... his arms full of buffalo robes. Without speaking Tall-Eagle mounted the sagging pony then silently began to ride out. When they reached the front of the line, Left-Wing and Blue-Leaf appeared with their own ponies... ready to accompany Tall-Eagle and the scout.

The Deer-Lady watched as Tall-Eagle conversed with Left-Wing... his arm gesturing in her general direction. Left-Wing followed his arm movement... and almost instantly locked eyes with her.

Instantly she averted her eyes. But when she looked up again, Left-Wing was coming towards her. Tall-Eagle, Blue-Leaf, and the scout rolled out far ahead... passing like shadows in the bright light of the sun into the folds of the land. Although she had witnessed their capacity for bravery and courage... still she sent a silent prayer on the wind towards them.

Passing over many hills... Tall-Eagle began to see the giant birds of ill omen gliding on motionless wings far off in the distance. Birds that feed upon the flesh of the dead. Although he had been told nothing... seeing the many decaying-flesh-eaters caused his already heavy heart to sink with sorrow and despair.

As they rounded the top of the next hill... a figure of a man on top of the horse came into view. From his stature, he knew it was Rising-Star. He sat motionlessly as the vultures circled high above... gracefully swimming on celestial currents. And as they moved even closer... Tall-Eagle painfully saw why.

Laying before the Rising-Sun was the body of a young warrior. His body had been ravaged by carnivorous wildlife... his entrails half-eaten... laying in the hollow emptiness of his rib cage. His mouth was open in a soundless scream of anguish as flies crawled over his unfeeling flesh. His eye sockets were empty... a feast for the birds overhead.

From atop of his horse... Tall-Eagle looked down towards the decaying corpse. In his chest was a black-feathered arrow. All around the corpse were many black-feathered arrows... some intact... others broken with the tip missing. Tall-Eagle knew these were the arrows of the Crow... from the black feathers to the thickness of the shaft... heavy and powerful.

"It is our messenger Red-Bear," Rising-Star said. "And the arrow belongs to the Crow." His words were spoken quietly... slipping out from a hardened mouth.

Tall-Eagle knew who it was... but said nothing... for it was he who sent both Red-Bear and Charging-Elk out seeking allied tribes... to warn of the forth coming war. And in doing so... he sent them out to their early deaths.

"We have yet to find Charging-Elk," Rising-Star said... as if reading the mind of Tall-Eagle. "But we have yet to search thoroughly... for I stayed to keep the vultures at bay.

"Perhaps he made it to the Oglala People," Big-Scout said... his voice tight with hope.

"You and Big-Scout go and find Charging-Elk. Blue-Leaf and I will wrap Red-Bear in a robe and sing the prayers for his journey." Tall-Eagle then looked up at the two scouts. Rising-Star face was serene... the attribution of hardened warriors... so evident by the ability to conceal painful emotions… so that none of his inner turmoil would show. Even so… the two rode off in silence.

Small, canine-carnivorous creatures watched the men from the outer fringes of an invisible circle… yelping and screaming at the men for interfering with their meal. Tall-Eagle leaned over the corpse… his tomahawk was still in his hand… broken on one side and crusted with dried blood. He reached down and lifted the stiffened arm… he had to unwrap the fingers which gripped the weapon one by one.

After he and Blue-Leaf have finished their task… he thoroughly surveyed the scene. All about him were the signs of a violent conflict… which laid in stark contrast to the soft beauty of the grass… which rustled a joyous tune as it swayed in the wind. Even the brush merely whispered as the tender fingers of the wind caressed the earth. But even in that beauty, he knew there was dry blood. His heart sank at the thought of him sending his people into an ambush.

At that very moment… a dark and sinister thought had struck the acting chief. Right now he stood far beyond the lands of the Crow… at least three suns journey. Yet before him lies Crow arrows. It stood to reason Red-Bear and Charging-Elk had been followed since day one… only to be stalked and murdered once at a great distance. But the question that ate away at his mind was rather or not the group who left with In-The-Woods were followed as well? And if so… what fate had become of them?

Question upon painful question raked his mind. He knew he was being stalked at that very moment. Perhaps by the very ones who sent Red-Bear to the Land-of-the-Spirits. It made their perilous way even more dangerous. To be watched and stocked by an unseen enemy… to face possible ambush at every turn by vengeful Crow… all the while fighting against doubts and uncertainty… fighting against loss and pain. Not one of the surrounding tribes even knew they lay at the very hands of open war.

Before they could see him… they heard the hoof beats of Big-Scout's pony. When they reached Tall-Eagle… the acting chief could see the pain behind his eyes.

"We found Charging-Elk. Rising-Star is with him now to keep the scavengers of dead flesh away."

"Crow?" Blue-Leaf asked… already knowing the answer.

"Crow," Big-Scout echoed somberly.

Tall-Eagle handed Big-Scout the remaining buffalo robes and said, "Blue-Leaf and I will remain here, send Charging-Elk's spirit home in a good way… then return, bring his body with you. Before nightfall Left-Wing should be arriving.

Big-Scouts took the heavy robes then rode off in the direction of what he came… leaving behind Tall-Eagle, Blue-Leaf, and the mutilated vessel that was once Red-Bear.

Tall-Eagle's eye kept to the hills… his bow in hand. Blue-Leaf was a fine warrior. But with unknown numbers of enemies lurking in unknown places… the odds he faced are no doubt stacked against him. His senses must be on full alert.

"Perhaps we should prepare for the arrival of Left-Wing," Blue-Leaf stated. "They may not arrive until after the sun sets."

"Perhaps you are right, Blue-Leaf. Although our enemies are unseen… They are here. Let us keep this in mind as we prepare the site." Tall-Eagle then dismounted his pony and spiked it to the ground. Together they gathered enough materials for a small fire. Materials consisting of dry grass and harden buffalo dung.

Using his flint knife, he dug a deep fire pit into the prairie so that the flame would be low. A low flame sparingly kindled wouldn't create a highly visible back light which could be used to provide easy targets. Since their first surprise attack… caution was in order.

Blue-Leaf heard a small rustling in the soft layer of grass. Upon further investigation, he spotted a plump hare. In a fluid motion, he reached for an arrow from the quiver strapped to his back…. fitted the feathered end and released it in the blink of an eye.

The arrow was swift and true… and the rabbit was fastened to the ground. Before long Big-Scout and Rising-Sun returned with the remains of Charging-Elk… his body tightly wound with braided strands of willow bark. As they awaited the arrival of Left-Wing… they all sat in awkward silence. Their hearts heavy… remembering the two warriors who have fallen in battle at this very place.

"They fought as well," Raising-Star said reassuringly. "The lance of Charging-Elk was coated with dry blood and hair."

"Red-Bear's quiver was empty. And his tomahawk was broken," Blue-Leaf said softly as he chuckled grimly.

"Indeed, they fought well," Rising-Star repeated.

When the party of Left-Wing arrived… the sun was just beginning to sink beyond the western hills along the horizon… sending flaming colors that raced brilliantly across the open skies. The moments Tall-Eagle saw the Deer-Lady… he felt the butterflies from within flutter their soft wings. Still, she walked beside his horse and the pony-drag which carried the body of No-Horns.

To the Deer-Lady, Tall-Eagle raised his hand in greetings. She followed suit… raising her own hand and slyly bowing her head. But they didn't speak. Aside from the small gestures, one would have easily missed the subtleties of budding emotions flowing between the two.

Tall-Eagle watched as Left-Wing and Little-Bull approached. "They have gathered in numbers. But they maintain a respectable distance from my far-reaching bow," Left-Wing said laughing as he pointed towards the rear of the camp.

There Tall-Eagle saw a small band of Crow warriors… Numbering 24 in all. Even at that distance he could see their horses were of great stature… strong… powerful… and nicely groomed. Their coats glistening in the fires of a setting sun. Their long tails swished back and forth as they hooved at the ground. Their manes were neatly braided on their thick next. And the warriors who sat upon them sat tall and proud… their faces brightly painted with colors of war.

Tall-Eagle then looked at his own rugged ponies as Yellow-Horse and Big-Nose gathered them to care for them. It was a sad sight. Only he possessed a warhorse… all others were work-ponies on the verge of collapse. But his own horse had the heavy burden of transporting No-Horns… And it seemed to him the load was beginning to take its toll on his old friend.

"They must rest as we do," Left-Wing said. "We move slow because our ponies are worn. They track us easily because their horses are great. Tonight, let us make away with their horses," he said as he looked to the distant warriors and their steeds.

"Red-Bear and Charging-Elk are no more," Tall-Eagle said in a sad voice. Left-Wing's turned his dark eyes back to the acting chief... eyes that flashed with raw anger.

"So help will not arrive?" Left-Wing asked... his tone had turned hard.

"I think not," Tall-Eagle responded in a voice thick with sadness.

"What of In-The-Woods and his band?" Little-Bull asked... thinking of his wife and young son... a son who has yet to witness of full winter's count.

Tall-Eagle said nothing... for he knew nothing. "Perhaps we should gather in council," he said finally... wanting each warrior to carefully weigh the options that lay before them. "Let us finish making camp, then gather in the lodge of White-Sun."

There were scattered "a-ho," then each man took to work.

"Will you join us?" Tall-Eagle asked the Deer-Lady... who had stood in silence.

"Are women permitted in council?" she asked.

"Are they not where you are from?"

The Deer-Lady didn't respond to the question. Instead, she went to work wherever she could help. Tall-Eagle did as well. As he moved about the camp, he paid careful attention to avoid White-Sun, for he had an irrational fear that she would read what he kept hidden in his thoughts.

While Tall-Eagle was trying to avoid this imagine accusatory stare, the Deer-Lady was doing all she could to avoid Left-Wing. Although she had come to learn of his mischievous and dark humor... she still felt the burning sensation of negative energy radiating from this young warrior. To her, the sensation was closely akin to coming into physical and emotional contact with a dark start... she could feel her own energy slowly being drained.

Darkness fully conquered the Great-Plains when the Little-Star-Band finally settled in. An oppressive veil had laid gently over the band. The two latest deaths and its significance took its toll upon the group morale. They realized no help would be arriving. They were on their own.

After carefully assessing his People and their ponies… with a grim realization he came to see that both his People and their ponies were being pushed to the brink of collapse and/or exhaustion. He knew they were all in desperate need of a long rest.

Again, he felt torn. With the deaths of No-Horns… and now Red-Bear and Charging-Elk… it was more of a burden then the horses could bear. But he knew he couldn't bury his brothers here, for the Crow would no doubt desecrate the sacred grounds.

"I was told to inform you of a river just north of here," Blue-Leaf, said breaking his train of thought. The young warrior stood before the acting chief with an air of honor and pride. The swelling of his left I was receding, but his arm was still wrapped in a crude sling. "This wound will heal long before my pride," he said speaking of his arm when he realized Tall-Eagle was looking at his injuries. "Soon I will be able to count coup again."

"It seems the one they call Red-River has reason to fear," Tall-Eagle said as a sly grin slashed across his heart and mouth.

"Indeed he does. I have learned much from our first encounter," he said… speaking on how Red-River had pummeled him. "I now know his greatest weakness. I know his fears." Blue-Leaf then dropped his voice to a confidential whisper. "I know his weakness for it is his fear. He fear losing," he said as he pointed to his bruised face. "This knowledge will ensure my next victory."

Tall-Eagle unexpectedly howled with genuine laughter. "My young friend is wise behind beyond his years," he said as he put a caring hand on the young warriors back. "Red-River indeed has much to fear."

It wasn't very long before the weary band had laid out… ready to submit to sleep. Again the Deer-Lady had found herself in the lodge of White-Sun and Mocking-Bird. Again Tall-Eagle took the first watch… guarding against the direction of the ever-persistent Crow.

Before him… the lush valley was nothing more than of vast obscure void… silent and gray under the young moon… betraying nothing of the dangers that lie lurking within. The young moon was glimmering high above the heavens but gave off a little light for thin clouds waft before it. The stars were veiled as well.

Suddenly, Tall-Eagle felt unimaginably alone. He pulled his buffalo robe tight around his shoulders and psychologically prepared himself for an emotional onslaught... he knew that soon the voice of his memory will be there to taunt him.

He shuttered in the darkness. A cold darkness where he felt so alone... alone against imagined bloodhounds.

At that very moment, the Mayan step out into the pale light of the spring night. White-Sun had shot her with a disapproving stare, for they both knew where she was going. But the Deer-Lady simply ignored the woman's harsh glare.

Instantly, she was greeted by the chill of the night. She took the soft fur of the elf-skin blanket and settled it artfully about her shoulders. She went towards the direction of Tall-Eagle. She knew where he would be located... standing guard against those who wish to do her harm. At the thought... she felt her heart weakened.

For years, this lost Mayan had steeled her heart against the harsh realities of a cruel world. Knowing nothing but pain and distrust, she refused to let anyone near her although her heart remained open to all. A daunting paradox. She was brimming with love. A strong love. A powerful love. She was loving. Caring. Her heart was pure... and open to those willing and receptive. But there was a barrier... an inner sanctum which could not be penetrated. And for this place... this inner sanctum, she felt herself becoming vulnerable. Vulnerable to Tall-Eagle

Slowly, she made her way towards the east. The half-moon gave off a small amount of light. Tall-Eagle was lost in the dark shadows of the night. In a soft voice, she called out his name.

Her words... his name... fluttered in the heart of Tall-Eagle. At first, he wondered if his mind was playing a cruel trick upon his wanting heart. Perhaps the loneliness was becoming more than he could bear. Deep within... he knew he wanted her... needed her... he needed to be with her... not only for that lonely and vulnerable moment... but forever.

Terrible things had happened that led them together. So many lives had been lost. So much pain. Perhaps she needed him just as bad as he needed her? Not just physically against the vengeful Red-River. But perhaps she needed him emotionally and spiritually as well.

Again he heard his name being called from the lonely darkness... and again he felt his heart flutter.

He placed a hand over his lips and muffled his call... a call that mimicked an owl.

The Mayan recognized it immediately. Smiling to herself... she followed the soft sounds.

To her surprise, she found Tall-Eagle sitting open and exposed, instead of taking refuge under the dark shadows of the tall grass. He sat under his robe with his arms wrapped around his legs. Beside him laid his tools of war.

"Should I fear the call of the bird-of-prey?" she asked as she gave one of her rare smiles. That smile that seemed to melt his heart each and every time.

"As long as my heart beats and my blood runs, you need never fear me or those around me, for I will do all I can to protect you."

"I believe you," she said softly and that husky voice.

Tall-Eagle then fell into an uncomfortable silence... afraid he was unwittingly revealing intimate details that should remain hidden deep within his heart.

"White-Sun disapproves of me being out here," she said quietly and safely, not wanting to voice how she truly felt about the situation.

"White-Sun is wise to the ways of our People. She holds our customs and laws to heart. And intimate contact between you and I is forbidden. This is why she disapproves of us being alone."

"Is it forbidden for me to join you and watch for Crow? Are they not my enemies as well?" she asked inarguably.

Before he could answer, she sat beside him in the soft grass. For a long time, they said nothing. But their minds and hearts were racing. They both were approaching unfamiliar, yet sacred grounds. "Tell me more of your people, tell me more of the Mayans," Tall-Eagle said, wanting to hear the voice of the Deer-Lady.

A thick cloud concealed the light of the moon as it drifted slowly at the heavens. She stared into the black void that seem to yawn before them like deep and cold space. She hadn't been with her People since that fateful day as a child. She remembered very little about her people. But every horrible detail about that day had vividly etched and burned itself upon her soul.

Instantly, she turned her mind away from those painful memories of her father and instead thought about how her people had felled the mighty trees of a dense jungle... how they cut a wide path and built stone-laid roads that reached out in all directions. These stone paths allowed all the Mayan people to travel and trade freely. She thought of how her people had built towering pyramids. Pyramids that rose above the tallest of trees in the surrounding jungle. She thought of how her people had charted the stars by carefully measuring their movements. She thought of all the things and beauty her people had created. All the accomplishments. The art. The science. Astronomy. Astrology. All the cultural and religious concepts. She then thought of how none of this remains. Everything is gone, shattered.

"I was married once," she said finally. "He was a pale-face, a white man," she asserted grimly.

She paused as she looked towards the heavens. From time to time the veil of clouds would part... allowing stars and the light of the moon to briefly shine through. Tall-Eagle looked down beside him at the Mayan. She had bundled herself against the early spring chill. She then drew her knees up to her chest to feel trap the warmth of her own body.

The way the pale moon limned her narrow face had caused his longing heart to yearn even more. But the broken sky wouldn't allow the light to last long. Again and again the heavens would lighting and then darken as clouds drifted lazily before the moon.

Tall-Eagle was a seasoned warrior. A warrior who had honed his skills at reading the subtle inclinations and tiny inflections of people. A skill needed when holding council with present and/or former enemies of the Sioux. As the Mayan spoke of her husband, he couldn't help but feel the hatred that slept just beneath the surface of her words. He wanted to push her for information... but quickly discovered there was no need.

"His spirit was tainted by the greed of his race." Her husky voice had turned soft and hypnotic as she spoke against the rising breeze. "It was in his nature to set man against man, for he was an enemy of the natural world. I thought I could change this. Change him. I had visions of a paradise where the two races could thrive in peace and harmony. I had a dream where the mingling of the two races would bring the best of both worlds to a single point. A point that would perhaps be a shining example to all the nations across the world."

A hazy veil of tears burned her eyes as long-buried memories fought and clawed the way to the surface.

There was another part in the clouds. In the deep of night... under the hard lights of stars... the Mayan wept.

She hid her face with long, slender and graceful fingers. Tall-Eagle leaned against her... she instantly and naturally laid her head upon his hard shoulders. Just as naturally he place an arm about her shoulders. And there... he held her... feeling the strain of her delicate muscles slowly relax.

Leaning into Tall-Eagle... feeling his warmth, his heat, against the chill of the night and the aura of loneliness that had enveloped him caused her to weep all the more. She did not weep violently. She wept in that heartbroken way that only the longing could truly understand.

Surrounded by his warmth, her body continued to relax... slowly melting into his arms. She then closed your eyes and lifted her face towards the skies. Her face was washed in the thin, white light of the moon... the trail of tears sparkling like tiny stars. She sighed deeply as she lowered her head.

Sensing his own tears as they begin to sting his eyes, Tall-Eagle reached over and gently wisp away a tear.

"I was alone. I needed to feel safe. So I manufactured a kind of love I thought would bond me to him. But in our travels, I watch as his people went place to place, systemically pulling the natural resources from the people they conquered. The silver. The gold. Stealing and killing as they went. In the end, the forced love I managed to conjure had turned to poison, putrid in its artificiality."

Again she sighed deeply. She raised her head to look directly into the eyes of Tall-Eagle. "But still, a heart that brims with love longs to share. A heart that burns with love yearns for another heart that is pure. Do you agree, Tall-Eagle," she asked in a voice that had always seemed to envelop him with enchantment.

Tall-Eagle quickly turned away... suddenly hot with a bitter flash of memory. Memories of Girl-Lost. He tried to turn his mind away from his wife and the child that never was.

But it was too late. It's every bitter emotion came rushing to the surface. There was a steady stream of tears rolling from the warrior's eyes, though he made not a single sound. But it was this silent weeping that truly tore at the Mayan's heart.

"I once knew love," he said finally.

So many thoughts swam through his head. Old, haunting memories that seem so unrelenting in their agony. Several moments have passed before he spoke again.

The Mayan was shaking in her anticipation.

"The stars hold the story of my people, for the stars hold knowledge of all things," he said as he turned his gaze towards the heavens. "And if you know the songs of our hearts, you can read our stories in the night sky. The stars are the oldest and wisest beings in our existence. Their understanding of universal knowledge is without boundaries."

All Lakota children were told of the star path. Especially those belonging to the Little-Star-Band. He couldn't recall all the little antidotal stories from his childhood. Even if he could, he knew that generations had veiled the distinction between what is real and what is fantasy. He knows time has a way of eroding the limited boundaries of what humans perceive as reality. He also knows that a new star had appeared in the heavens the night his wife and child crossover.

"I was married to Gypsy-Angel, Girl-Lost. She was always happy, smiling. But deep within, there was a pain. Loneliness. A pain and loneliness I recognized instantly."

The Mayan laid a gentle hand upon his shoulder. The gesture was involuntary... a physical expression of the passion she felt rising deep within.

"Physically, she was the complete opposite of me. But our tortured hearts and souls had been forged in the same fires. The innocent beauty that was my Gypsy-Angel accepting me as I was. And she loved me. A love that filled me with a comfort that deepened with each day that passes. It filled my heart, my soul. It gave me peace." Again, he paused... his eyes searching the heavens for the star that had been Girl-Lost.

"I remember the day she told me she was with child. Never had I imagined I could feel such joy. Such happiness. I embraced my wife, and I held her like I've never held her before."

A slow and timid smile crossed his lips. "I dropped to my knees and place my ear against her stomach, whispering softly to my unborn child. As time passed, my wife got bigger and bigger." Tall-Eagle chuckled softly to himself as he said, "She ate as if she was giving birth to a baby buffalo. She was my heart. My love."

Then his look turned grim... solemn... dark eyes gazing out from deep and strange shadows of pain and sorrow. "The moment she cried out, I just knew with every fiber of my being she wouldn't make it. She laid hidden, in the dark shadows of my tipi. White-Sun heard her cries and came rushing to her aid. I dropped to my knees beside her, gently slipping a hand under her head and neck. Her flesh was glistening with sweat, her hair plastered to her temples as her face contorted with agonizing pain. Everything else became a blur," he said, his voice trembling with raw emotions. "I couldn't hear anything. All I saw was blood. My wife's blood.

"Her eyes were clenched shut as she cried out a silent scream. The tears were streaming from the corner of her eyes. White-Sun was shouting at Mocking-Bird, but I heard nothing. The sticky blood that coated both their arms held grim evidence of what I knew to be true in my heart. But still, I prayed. I prayed with every ounce of my being. I prayed with all the strength I could muster. I prayed.

"Then my wife looked at me. Her soft brown eyes were wide and troubled, searching my face for some tiny hint of hope. Searching my face for some tiny hint of reassurance. But I couldn't give that to her. I couldn't do anything but stare. She whispered something. But I couldn't hear her. She laid her head against my arm. I felt her nails digging weakly into my flesh. Then her hand dropped and her head fell from my arm.

"White-Sun held my child to her chest. Her entire front a washed in my wife's blood. And there, in her arms was a tiny baby. She held it. Globs of sticky hair was plastered against his tiny head. Its tiny body was streaked with a type of white foamy lather and red blood. But it wasn't moving. His arms and legs were limp. Its head rolled as if its neck had been broken. It's tiny face pinched and deep purple. Again, I prayed. I prayed to the Great-Spirit. I pray to the spirits of my ancestors. I prayed, please, just give me my child. I begged. I pled. I screamed and I cried, please let my child live. And for a brief moment, I thought I saw its tiny fists clench. Clenched as if fighting to live. Fighting to stay with me. But it was only hope. Lonely, desperate hope. My son had left. My life was no more. I was ready to die."

His voice trailed off at the last part. But there was so much desperation in his voice. The kind of desperate rage directed at the cruelty of life. Again, she placed her head on his shoulder... her heart bleeding for this proud warrior who had endured so much.

That night, under the harsh light of soft stars... Tall-Eagle allowed himself to weaken... unmasked by the soft and innocent beauty of the Mayan. His warrior persona, his hard exterior, now betrayed by the steady flow of tears that welled from a tortured soul.

"That day I cursed the Great-Spirit. I had become so full of raw anger and hatred, I curse the very essence of the Great-Spirit. Blaming the Creator for destroying all that I had ever loved. All that I had ever had a chance to love. But that night a new star had appeared in the heavens. A star nobody had ever witnessed before. I thought it was her. I just knew it was her. It has vanished as suddenly as it appeared. Each night I would search the skies, looking for my beloved wife and child. It was like the Great-Spirit was giving me one last chance to say goodbye to them both."

"Where is it? The star?" the Mayan acquired as she looked up at Tall-Eagle... the pale white light of the half-moon glistened off wet traces on her thin cheeks.

"It was there," he said as he lifted a finger to a dark void and between two star clusters. "Still I prayed to this darkness. Praying my Gypsy-Angel would hear my voice." He then began to speak in an ancient dialect of Lakota... a language unknown by even the eldest of the Lakota People.

Even from the language, the Mayan heard from the others, instantly she knew his words were different. It seemed to be Lakota... but it was a soft and poetic language that registered only to her soul. "That was so beautiful, Tall-Eagle," she whispered when he had finished... deeply affected by this display of human weakness.

"This is the prayer of my heart, my soul. The voice I have sent may be weak, but I sent it with every fiber of my being."

The stars slowly crept across the heavens in a wide and silent ark. The two had long ago felled into silence... content simply to listen to the two desperate hearts beating in the quiet darkness.

The Mayan was the first to be conquered by sleep. Her shyness had vanished this night and the ambitions to uphold the strict boundaries that forbade them from physical contact was gone. She fell asleep with her head upon his warm chest... listening to the soft thumping of his heart.

As she laid upon his chest, he watched as a gentle sleep crept upon her. Every muscle in his body was cramped and throbbing with tension. But he willed himself not to move. He was afraid to move. Afraid of waking her. Afraid of losing this moment.

In her sleep... her delicate features betrayed nothing of the cruelty of her life or how this life had greatly wronged her. She seems so peaceful... so tranquil... he wanted this moment to last forever.

Half the night had come and gone... and the time had come for all of them to switch guards. He heard his replacement before he saw him. But Tall-Eagle didn't want to break the enchanting spell he now felt.

Brave-Shield was silently taken aback when he stumbled upon the two. In the dim starlight, he saw that the Mayan was asleep. Tall-Eagle said nothing. There was no need. A knowing smile play upon the lips as the young warrior. He then began to gently lay the Buffalo robe softly over the two quiet forms. "Stay," he whispered softly so that he wouldn't disturb the sleeping Mayan. "Find sleep, my friend. I will stand guard further down the hill."

With this, the young warrior, along with his tools of war, stealthily crept towards the east.

Tall-Eagle allowed himself to slowly relax... moving only in stages... until finally, he laid fully on his back. The Mayan still slept... her head still upon his chest. His every cramped muscle cried out in anger. But his heart knew it was all worthwhile.

The eastern skies beyond the distant hills were taking on its first pinkish tinge when the Mayan had opened her eyes. Through sleep clouded eyes she looked about her. All around her the ground was soft and wet. A deep chill penetrated her flesh as the morning air touched her bare shoulders. I thin mist seemed to cover the grass... glimmering in the fading rays of a falling moon. It was cold.

She pulled the buffalo robes tighter around herself and a sleeping Tall-Eagle. She then nuzzled against his arm and chest... seeking the warmth of his embrace. She found that his flesh was hot to the touch. Feeling this heat radiating from the sleeping warrior caused another shiver to tear violently through her. But there was comfort in his warmth.

She has spent many nights sleeping open and exposed to the elements. She has slept beneath the stars in the high country... has slept in the lowlands, hidden amongst thickets of scrubs cedars. No matter how many nights she spent sleeping out in the open, she didn't think she would ever get used to the morning chill.

Her mind turned to the sleeping man that laid beside her. She was all too familiar with loneliness. All too familiar with the longing of a lonely heart.

The purple hue of dawn that kindled the eastern skies continued to grow... slowly dwarfing the beauty of the Morning-Star. The smell of fire smoke filled the cold morning air as the Little-Star-Band slowly came to life. The grassy plains embraced the first rays of the sun... flares of golden beams creating a pinkish hue that caressed the distant heels ever so delicately. All around her was open prairie... dotted by gray shadows of hills whose face was awashed in beautiful morning colors.

Tall-Eagle began to stir in his sleep. The Mayan grew silent, not wanting to rise him from his peaceful sleep. But it was of no use, the warrior instantly became fully aware of her presents. The buffalo robes was raked over their shoulders… it was then she noticed her head was upon his bare chest. She went to pull it away, breaking the physical contact. But seeing the flicker of regret in her eyes, he clasped her fingers in his and held it against his body. The heat radiating from his body penetrated her soul.

The Mayan gave the Lakota a shy glance before she lowered her head. Tall-Eagle repositioned himself on his elbow so that he may look upon the Mayan fully. "There is no need for modesty now," he said with a smile. "For you fell asleep with your head upon my chest. Already, the laws have been broken."

With her head still down, the Mayan raised only her eyes to look at him… a slow and rare smile seemed to play upon her thin lips. A smile that illuminated his world.

Every single time the Mayan would smile, the hardened warrior could feel his heart flutter within his chest. She didn't smile that often, her expression was always like his, rather serious and often grim. But the soft and gentle smile she now displayed had reminded the warrior how attached he had become to her, and how much he needed her, how much he depended on her.

The morning sun seemed to dance upon the hilltops towards the east. The band camp-site was alive with activities as each went about doing their chores. A cool dampness crept up from the creek, the smell of fresh water seemed inviting. Together, the Mayan and the Lakota started walking towards the creek.

White-Sun stood towards the center of the camp… watching as the two walked down the hill. Incidentally, she saw how close to each other they walked, at times their shoulders would brush against each other. She knew that deep within, hidden beneath layers of bitterness and frustration, the two loved each other. She also knew that soon his love will surface, and the emotions they felt for each other will be realized. But she also knew Tall-Eagle will never allow anything to come of it. No matter how deep the emotions, Tribal Law would never allow it, he knew it.

So sad, she thought bitterly to herself, *love is a gift from the Creator. A gift Tall-Eagle could never share.*

The two walked beside the sparkling stream, stopping at a spot where the fast currents nibbled at the sandy shore. Swallows and mourning doves played in the small puddles, whistling the morning cheer to awaken the world. All about them was a magical world... a realm of peace and tranquility.

He watched as the Mayan knelt beside the flowing stream. With gentle fingers, she cupped the water and brought a handful out. Slowly she parted her fingers and allow the water to slip through. Like giant raindrops, the water fell back into the stream.

"I find peace when I am with you," she said as she watched the water fall between her fingers. "I find comfort when I am with you."

"As do I," Tall-Eagle said as he knelt beside her. "You have heard the secrets of my heart. You have felt the yearning in my spirit. No other soul can make such a claim."

"Well it seems as if we both are vulnerable to each other," the Mayan said as she ran her fingers gently across the top of the water.

"I fear that I have made myself more vulnerable than you. Yet, this is something I do not fear," Tall-Eagle said barely above a whisper.

At that moment a shrilling war cry ripped through the air. The Mayan flinched at the sudden screech.

Being snapped back to reality Tall-Eagle sprang to his feet and turned his attention towards the makeshift camp. In an instant Left-Wing appeared with weapons in hand.

"The Crow continue to torment us," Left-Wing growled as he gripped his weapon tightly.

"I know you hunger for war, my young friend. But now is not the time. Our time will come soon enough. Let us continue to break camp," Tall-Eagle said to his warrior.

Without another word being spoken, Left-Wing turned from the two and headed back towards the camp.

Throughout the day the Little-Star-Band traveled on word... their bodies screaming for rest... their spirits screaming for peace. But still, they solemnly marched onward. Before long the group stood upon a bluff overlooking the vast prairie. For below in the valley... tall grass swayed and rippled in the soft wind... steady bellowing and castigating like a green ocean. The wild buffalo dotted the valley below. Tall-Eagle turned his face towards the high sun. Thick clouds dotted the vastness of the heavens. A soft breeze caressed his face as he prayed silently for peace.

"I smell rain on the wind," Brave-Shield said to Tall-Eagle as he went to stand next to him.

"As do I," stated Tall-Eagle in a low voice. "Soon we will be at the top of the next hill, and then we shall see."

Far to the west... dark clouds blanketed the heavens... and on the breeze came the soft scent of rain. Tall-Eagle silently reprimanded himself for not paying closer attention to the signs of bad weather... his mind had been absorbed by the Crow that followed as their numbers steadily grew.

In the distance... upon a gentle slope stood a forest of trees. The trees were thick and black against the gray sky. It seemed to him that both night and the coming storm will greet them simultaneously. So he opted for the soft dryness of the trees.

Tall-Eagle re-directed the group towards the line of trees. A bitter chill came into the moist air as the scent of rain became heavy. The dark clouds of the west was making its way east... bringing with it a terrible storm. Gentle thunder rolled over the prairie from the west. Slowly the sky faded into a cold gray. The trees stood mournfully before them... dark and somewhat foreboding. Their heavy leaves hanging limp... softly rustling in the chill of the westerly wind.

Upon reaching the tree-line, Tall-Eagle sent Rising-Star and Big-Scout to canvas the surrounding area. As they awaited their return Yellow-Horse and Big-Nose began to unpack the ponies so that they may care for the exhausted and fatigued creatures. Left-Wing and Blue-Leaf... whose job it was to bring up the rear rode towards the acting chief.

"Their numbers continue to grow," Left-Wing informed Tall-Eagle. "By their attire and war-bonnets... I believe they are the people of Arikara."

To Tall-Eagle... Left-Wing's expression revealed something more than an inner pain of loss and the overriding desire for vengeance. He believed he saw in the stoic warrior a small flicker of fear, for the number of their enemies is becoming overwhelming. "How many?" he finally asked.

"At least a hundred Arikara warriors have joined the ranks," Blue-Leaf said as he lowered his head in grim resignation.

"Their numbers are greater than ours. Why do they not attack?" Pretty-Elk said... more of a thought than a question.

"The Arikara aren't Warriors. They may mimic the battle cries and war-song of warriors. They may even be expert horseman. But they are not true warriors. Not in the Lakota sense." Left-Wing said superbly masking the new fear that lingered in his look. In fact... there seems to be laughter just beneath the surface of his words. "And the Crow will not attack because they know this as well." Again, Tall-Eagle sensed the smirk lining his tone and saw just a hint of amusement return to his dark eyes.

Before long Rising-Star and Big-Scout return. "All is clear," Big-Scout said. "Rising-Star even shot a deer. If we hurry, White-Sun and Mocking-Bird can have the meat stripped before the rain comes."

"This is good," Tall-Eagle said. Again he looked at the Deer-Lady... her soft brown eyes seemed to be watching his every move. Suddenly he felt dirty... unclean and rugged from the hard journey. "Take them to the kill," he instructed the two scouts in an effort to erase the unpleasant thought. With this being said, Rising-Star and Big-Scout went to find White-Sun and Mocking-Bird. He then turned to Left-Wing and Blue-Leaf and said, "Keep an eye on the Crow and their allies."

"Come," he said to Big-Rock and Blue-Stalk, "let us find a site within the woods before night falls and the rain is upon us."

In expert fashion... the band of nomads were able to erect a campsite in a short amount of time. Tipis were erected and lean-tos were fashioned using raw materials scavenged from the woods. White-Sun and Mocking-Bird had returned and was smoking venison on a low burning flame within her lodge. The darkness had fallen over the land... like a suffocating blanket. The land had grown dark... for the stars were hidden behind the rain clouds.

Rolling thunder continued to creep towards the east... low and distant at first. But growing with strength and intensity. There was soft whining amongst the horses as they stomped nervously against the ground.

Then the rain came. Soft at first. But they knew from the dancing bolts of lightning in the distance that the worst was yet to come.

Tall-Eagle helped as the last lodge poles were being set... then they were quickly covered with a thick hide. Everything was finished long before the heavy rains came.

Tall-Eagle has sent paired warriors to stand guard. Left-Wing and Blue-Leaf to the east... Brave-Shield and Bad-Claw to the South... Little-Bull and Big-Rock to the west and Rising-Sun and Big-Scout to the north.

The once distant mutter of thunder began to boom across the sky. The wind picked up in strength and power... the raindrops became fat and round. A blinding bolt of lightning ripped across the angry black sky. The air became thick... charged with electricity that caused the short hairs on the gape of his neck to rise. Many of the warriors who didn't have tipis abandon their lean-tos in search of lodges to share. Despite the desire, he knew he couldn't seek shelter.

Fighting against the wind and rain... Tall-Eagle made his way to the lodge of White-Sun. Upon entering he found White-Sun, Mocking-Bird, and the Deer-Lady... along with the two warriors Dog-Chief and Turns-Black... refugees from the gathering storm.

White-Sun and Mocking-Bird was doing the best they could to prepare food for the entire camp within the confinements of the lodge. The stench of venison and roasting rabbit was thick in the cramped lodge. All but the Deer-Lady seemed not to mind... who grimaced against the smell and was swallowing hard to rid her slender throat of the acrid smoke.

"I am here for those who stand point," Tall-Eagle said to White-Sun...

who in turn nodded her head at Mocking-Bird. Tall-Eagle then looked across the fire to the Deer-Lady. Seeing her struggle against the stench and smoke cause him to smile inwardly to himself. "The lodge I am now using is open to you, if this is what you wish," he said to her.

This caused White-Sun's head to snap to attention. In the flickering light of the fire he could see her eyes glaring intensely at him. He knew she was a traditionalist and thought it very inappropriate for a man and a woman to share a lodge if they were not married. Tall-Eagle said nothing of the icy glare... for it would only set her off in one of her volatile tirades.

"You have seen the dream symbols on the lodge of In-The-Woods, you know which one it is. You will find three other warriors including Pretty-Elk there," he said in an attempt to soothe White-Sun's anxieties. He then took the strips of meat from Mocking-Bird and exited the lodge.

Thunder roared as lightning streaked the heavens in mad flashes. He pulled his robe tightly about him as he fought against the rain and wind. With the moon and starlight concealed behind boiling clouds, it was a struggle for Tall-Eagle to find the warriors within the darkness. He found the first two huddled mournfully together under the thick brush... shivering terribly in their blankets and robes. Tall-Eagle handed the two their portion of venison and asked if they knew who the replacements were.

They said they did, so he made his way to the next two. Passing through the darkness of the trees, he made his way to the clearing of which his guards were on point. They sat in the hollow of a dead tree... quiet and fully alert... watching through the coldness of wind and rain. Again he provided their portions and inquired about their replacements. He repeated the process with the third pair and made his way to the location of Left-Wing and Blue-Leaf.

Of course, the two were well hidden in the thick undergrowth of an old tree. Tall-Eagle had walked by the hiding pair twice... which Left-Wing thought to be amusing. On the third pass, Blue-Leaf called out from the shadows with soft tones. With soft laughter, the two shadows detach themselves from an even greater darkness.

"The storm seems to be passing," Tall-Eagle said in the silence that followed a boom of thunder. He then handed their portion of meat and said to Blue-Leaf, "when the time comes, find me in my lodge and I shall take your place at point."

At that very moment the world exploded with living light as a bolt of lightning touched the earth. The earth seemed to tremble under its touch as thunder cracked overhead. The power of the bolt and thunder caused his heart to skip a beat as his chest grew tight.

Just then Left-Wing began to chuckle. "Perhaps guards aren't needed. I'm sure their hearts would be small and frightened within this storm."

Tall-Eagle laughed slightly at the irony.

Tall-Eagle approach the place where the horses were kept... he could hear their desperate whines on the wind. He found Yellow-Horse and Big-Nose doing their young best to soothe the frightening beast who fought noisily against their harnesses... trying to free themselves so that they may flee from the deafening thunder.

The heavy winds, thunder, and lightning had passed when Tall-Eagle reached his lodge. But the rain continued to fall mercilessly from the dark heavens. Tall-Eagle quickly entered the lodge... drawing close the elk-skin across the door... shutting out the harshness of the night. He was surprised to find the Deer-Lady sitting alone... tending to the fire that burned warmly in the very center.

Tall-Eagle felt himself shiver against the sudden warmth... but found the sensation very pleasant.

Tall-Eagle was peripherally aware of the Deer-Lady watching him from across the fire as he removed his wet robe and hung it on a makeshift peg. But she remained silent. After he finished he sat before the fire with his own portion of deer meat and begin to eat in silence.

For some reason, the acting Chief found himself fighting the urge to question the whereabouts of the warriors whom he shared the lodge with. Perhaps it was the weight of the prolonged silence that began to unnerve him. But he felt something needed to be said to break the heavy silence between them. But it was the Deer-Lady who spoke first.

She reached across the fire and tried handing Tall-Eagle another portion of venison bound in leather. "I eat very little. And I see you work tirelessly," she said as she held the token out.

He looked from the venison to her eyes... they reflected the dancing flames of the fire. He knew it would be disrespectful not to gracefully accept the gift... so he didn't allow his reluctance to show.

As he took the meat bound in leather... his hand briefly met hers. And in that brief moment, he felt her tremble. Rather she trembled at his touch or to the chill of the night... he wasn't sure. But still, it caused his own heart to flutter wildly in his chest. Again he looked at the dancing flames in her eyes... oh how he wished to draw from the light and warmth of that eternal flame. But again... he kept his emotions well hidden.

Quickly she withdrew her hand and sat back on her heels with her legs beneath her. She stared humbly into the fire in an attempt to avoid eye contact. "Thank you," he said quietly.

"It is I who should be thanking you, Tall-Eagle," she said in that husky voice.

Again they fell into a heavy silence. He watched her in the dim light of the fire. He watched her narrow face... soft and golden. Softer than strands of sunlight filtering through clouds in the heavens at sunset. More golden than the suns first light at morning's dawn. How lucky she must feel to have skin that glows in the night... like soft flames... like magic. He thought of her as some mythological creature from stories of old. Her serious demeanor... her rare smile... her thick hair with more hues of brown than a forest. She could have been an enchantress... for any man who were to look upon her would be captivated by her strange and anomalous beauty.

As he watched her he began to wish she could hear his thoughts. Wishing he could cast his thoughts into her mind so she could see what was in his heart.

The Deer-Lady look up from the fire and saw as Tall-Eagle ate the last bit of the venison. She placed another small bundle of twigs on the fire then drew her knees up to her chin... wrapping her arms around her legs. "I have observed your heart," she said unexpectedly.

"And what did you see?" he asked as his interest peeked.

She looked him in his sad eyes. But behind those same eyes burned smoldering fires of true love. A true love and a stoic resolved to see his people through the perils and struggle of their journey. "I see the greatest of warriors," she said softly in the near husky-voiced.

Tall-Eagle chuckled slightly. "I am not even the best warrior in this small clump of trees, let alone the best in the Little-Star-Band. "

"You hear my words, Tall-Eagle. But you do not feel them. You are the greatest of warriors because you are the most gentle of men."

His heart swelled with pride at her words and again he found himself melting in her presents. "My heart flutters in my chest. Is this the trait of a warrior?" he said as he tried laughing away the comment.

"I believe it is," she responded.

Wanting to change the subject he asks, "What is your sign?"

"My sign?" she asked confusingly.

"Are you not a believer in the zodiac?" he said as he smiled mysteriously.

"How do you know of such things?" she asked... completely impressed.

He then told her how three summers ago he attended Council in the land of the Algonquian... and there was an elder from the Wampanoag tribe. And this elder had met and fell in love with a pale-face woman... a woman who believed in the Zodiac. And she taught this elder all about the star-path of the pale faces... who then told Tall-Eagle of these mysteries. "Are you a Pisces? A cancer?" he asked the Deer-Lady.

"No. I am a Libra," she said with a smile. Never had the warrior seen the Deer-Lady smile so much. "Taurus?" she asked Tall-Eagle... but Tall-Eagle just looked at her confusingly. "Gemini?"

"I don't understand," he admitted cautiously... not wanting to spoil the mood.

"Your sign? Are you a Taurus or Gemini?"

Slowly, a small timid smiled danced over his lips. "I don't know these words. Only Pisces and cancer and zodiac," he said shyly... trying to hold back a laugh. "I was told I am an Aquarius. But I don't know what that means," he said as the laughter finally spring forth... and the Deer-Lady laughed with him.

Slowly the conversation evolved as one topic naturally led to others. This was the first real conversation Tall-Eagle had with the Deer-Lady... a conversation that wasn't sad or sorrowful... a conversation that wasn't rigid or forced. She told him of her days growing up in two worlds... spending time in the white man's world... yet having that ancestral pride of the Mayan.

Tall-Eagle told her of his People, the Little-Star-Band, and how they spend their summers hunting buffaloes on the open prairies. And during the fall they would roam the Black-Hills for deer, elk, or moose. The children would gather seeds and dig for roots. They will pick fruits from the trees and hunt for berries. The older children caught fish and set rabbit snares while the women set up racks to smoke the fish and meat they didn't eat. And the elders would tell stories to the children as they dried berries for the coming winter.

As they talked, the soft crackle of the fire and a gentle tap of falling rain begin to lure the Deer-Lady to sleep. The weird play of light from the fire highlighted the long sweep of her neck... and again he would find himself wishing they were home so that he was free to speak his heart.

He watched as her eyelids grew heavy. "Do you remember that feather?" he asked... wanting it to be the last thing she thought about before falling into the realm of dreams. "Do you remember the feather with a white tip?"

"I do. Why do you ask?"

"I ask because it is yours. I will hold it until Tribal Law allows me to give it to you." They then lapsed into a deep silence, where the Deer-Lady eventually fell into a deep sleep.

On his side of the lodge, Tall-Eagle began to succumb to sleep when there was a slight shake of the door. In his dream-like state, he believed it was simply the rain. But then the elk-skin door was lifted and Blue-Leaf's had appeared. His face was dripping with rain... his long braids dripping steadily.

"It is time, Tall-Eagle," he said and then stepped back from the lodge.

After retrieving his flint knife... tomahawk... lance and his bow and arrows... he selected a dry buffalo robe and then stepped out into the wetness of the cold, rainy night. Both Blue-Leaf and Leaping-Fox were awaiting.

"A-ho," the two greeted the acting chief. "Is it not a good night for war?" Leaping-Fox said to Tall-Eagle.

"It is a good night for sleep," Blue-Leaf said, blinking against the rain. "I hear more thunder on the wind."

"As do I," Leaping-Fox agreed.

"Come," Tall-Eagle said to Leaping-Fox, "Let us relieve Left-Wing so that they may rest."

As they made their way to Left-Wing... they came across Pretty-Elk and Blue-Stalk now tending the horses.

"They are becoming restless again," Pretty-Elk said to Tall-Eagle. "I believe the Thunderbird will take flight again this night."

"Do you not hear the thunder on the wind?" Leaping-Fox ask.

"I hear nothing but water falling into my ears," Blue-Stalk joked.

The two then bid their farewells and headed to Left-Wing. Again he hid deep in the shadows. Already the sky was blacking by rain clouds... and again low thunder began to roll in from the west.

Left-Wing emerged from his place of concealment with a mischievous grin on his lips. "It seems the worst is yet to come," he said as he placed a hand on the shoulder of the acting chief. "If you need more rest, then I will stand guard, my old friend."

"Unless you need help falling asleep, my young friend, I believe you should remove your hand," Tall-Eagle responded and a joking manner.

"And who shall carry me all the way to my lodge once you lay me down to sleep? Or would you have me take my rest amongst nightcrawlers?" Left-Wing said in mock distress. "Besides, if you put me to sleep, who shall take all the glory if war were to happen this night?"

"Your words are so true, my friend. Your past glories will testify to the glories that has yet to come," Tall-Eagle said admiringly.

"So is the way of stories," Leaping-Fox said.

"So it is," said Tall-Eagle as he chuckled at the darkness of the humor. "Sleep well, Left-Wing, and Blue-Leaf. For tomorrow, travel will be difficult after a night of rain."

At this, the warriors departed and made their way back to the campsite while Tall-Eagle and Leaping-Fox settled into the moss-covered enclave of the dark underbrush. In the absence of moon and starlight... the world seemed to be shrouded in darkness. The thunder boomed overhead as quick flashes of lightning split the skies with jagged fingers. These flashes of light had cast long, flickering shadows that danced in the tree line... creating a sensation of ghostly apparitions lurking all about them.

Tall-Eagle griped his tomahawk with an unnatural strength... finding comfort with the weight of it in his hand. He looked over at Leaping-Fox... who crouched just outside of an arm's length beside him. Even so... in the darkness, all Tall-Eagle could see was a rough outline of the warrior.

Again a bolt of lightning had touched the earth... the earth seemed to tremble with rage as thunder shook the night.

His thoughts had turned towards the Deer-Lady... wondering if she could sleep through such noise. He knew he could. Once he knew what it was... he will grow accustomed to the sound... and allow the thunder to sing him to sleep. Even the sharp crack of thunder will be of little effect... for it all becomes white noise to him.

As he was thinking this... another flash of lightning branched the sky. And in that flash... Tall-Eagle caught a glimpse of a moving shadow in the electrician drama of the storm. But then everything fell back into darkness. As he awaited another flash of lightning he began to question whether or not he had even seen something to begin with.

But all doubts were erased... for in the flickering light of the storm he unmistakably spotted an enemy warrior as the intruder carefully stepped over a fallen tree branch. In his hands he held a flint knife and a tomahawk.

Tall-Eagle reached out and tap Leaping-Fox softly on the shoulder. He then pointed in the direction he saw the Crow scout... but the place had fallen into complete darkness.

"There is a scout there. Stay here." Tall-Eagle then emerged from the hiding place. As he moved stealthily across the slippery rocks, he withdrew his own flint knife... deciding to use it instead of a heavy tomahawk. His plan was to sneak up and render him harmless and unable to cry out an alarm... and a knife would work better for the task at hand.

Several incandescent flashes streaked across the heavens... lightening up his path as he made his way towards his enemy. Heavy rain fell on his body... causing him to shiver. But the adrenaline that burned in his veins easily pushed away the chill that tried penetrating his flesh.

Suddenly... the heavens became alive with another flash... and in this flash he saw many Crow warriors... moving through the trees like predatory beasts on the prowl. His heart began to pound in his chest as he thought of the overwhelming odds he and Leaping-Fox faced. The only thing he felt he could do was to yell out to his friend... who could then go and warn the camp.

Steeled with this resolved he let out a war cry... then launched at the closest Crow warrior to him. He caught the intruder by surprise as his flint knife penetrated his cold and wet flesh. The wounded warrior let out an agonizing cry that caught the attention of his Crow brethren.

Suddenly, the air was filled with the shrills of the enemy Crow.

The numerous Crow had overtaken Tall-Eagle with relentless and frightening rapacity. Stars and white light exploding behind closed eyelids as a lance crashed against the side of his head. Agonizing pain course the lengthening of his body as he staggered... his vision blurred as he fought to remain unconscious.

Tall-Eagle stuck out blindly with his tomahawk... he struck nothing but air. Again he was struck with a Crow lance... setting off more flashing lights behind his eyes.

Slowly, he felt himself falling. As he listened to the shrilling screams of Crow warriors he wondered if he was successful in his goal... providing Leaping-Fox with ample time to escape and warn the People? Or if his sacrifice was to be in vain. But soon his thoughts turn to the fire he felt being poured onto his back as lance blows rain down upon him. The rough stones underhand were wet and slippery from heavy rain... they felt cold against his flesh.

The Deer-Lady was jarred from a thin veil of sleep as the sound of cracking thunder ripped over the skies above. The small fire that laid before her were mere ambers that glowed dimly in the enveloping darkness. She always found herself shivering in those darkest hours just before the cold dawn of morning... the time when the air was at its coldest.

She added a few small twigs to the glowing embers then pulled weakly at the buffalo robe that made up her bed... the bed belonging to Tall-Eagle. As she thought about the warrior she tried desperately to find more warmth in his robes... pulling them up to just below her tiny chin.

Deep within she felt a soft stirring as she thought about him. A stirring caused by the butterflies in her stomach as they took flight. Within her heart she felt the merest of emotional whispers speaking softly to her soul.

The embers before her slowly turn into a small flame. Again she felt herself shivering against the cold.

Or was it?

The shiver felt violent... too much to be caused by chills. Suddenly, she felt a whisper of terror quicken her blood as a cold dread seem to embrace her. Something was wrong. She could feel it.

Slowly she emerged from the warmth of the robes and made her way to the door flap. The outside world laid in a blanket of darkness. The sound of heavy rain dampened all natural sounds. The heavens continue to be rocked by the Thunderbird as it continued to fire it's gaze upon the world. Natural and unnatural light became fused for the briefest of times as lightning flashed... illuminating the world all around her.

Again she felt a fierce shudder tear through her. She wanted to call out to the darkness... to Tall-Eagle. But she knew she wouldn't receive an answer. But out there... amid the rain... she sensed a movement in the tree line... a slight disturbance in the chaotic air.

At that moment she realized there was something evil lurking just beyond the clearing... she felt it... some demonic form... something darker than the other shadows of the forest... wanting nothing more than to harm her.

And then... as if on some sadistic cue... the dark heavens were seared by a blinding flash. A lightning bolt branched across the sky... and a white light lit the entire forest.

The Deer-Lady recoiled in unbridled horror as a row of ghostly figures flashed into being. They were off in the distance... between the trees... their features were twisted with a hunger to do violence.

She fought the instinctive emotional reaction to cry out in fear. Instead, she raced to the nearest lodge to raise them from their sleep. She rushed inside to find Turns-Black in a deep slumber.

"The Crow are here!" she whispered harshly as she fought to control the rising tide of fear threatening to wash over her.

Startled into full alertness, Turns-Black looked up at the Mayan in the soft glow of a low-burning fire.

Remember the language barrier... the Mayan simply grabbed his arm and pulled him towards the entrance of the lodge, putting her finger to her lips in a gesture for him to keep silent.

Peering out into the darkness, at first Turns-Black saw nothing. But in another flash of lightning, both he and the Deer-Lady could see the outlines of figures creeping along the clearing... like wicked shadows cascading out of the eerie darkness.

Turns-Black let out a piercing war cry... a cry so loud that it could be heard by all. The cry rang out above the thunder and noisy rain... a cry that projected an icy edge she had never knew.

The Crow began to yell their own battle cries as they swarm the soggy clearing like angry demons. The combined war whoops sent the remaining Lakota into action. Soon tipi flaps were being thrown open as the warriors emerged with weapons in hand. Many of them wore nothing more than a breechcloth.

"Go to the woods," Left-Wing instructed the Deer-Lady above the noise of the rain. "White-Sun and Mocking-Bird will find you when we are done here."

In the rush of excitement, more Lakota warriors headed towards the incoming Crow... ready to make this their last battle. Ready to kill... and ready to die. Soon the two opposing sides clashed in a heated battle of flint weaponry and blazing hatred.

The heavens refused to let up as the rain poured onto the battle. The Deer-Lady wanting to help where she can... but felt helpless in that moment. For brief moments the battlefield would come alive in the flash of lightning... but it was hard to tell whom was defeating who.

Suddenly her heart became heavy with sorrow... for her thoughts had suddenly turned to Tall-Eagle. The invading Crow had come from the direction of which he stood guard... and she knew he would never allow them to pass unchallenged. Her heart went out to the fallen warrior.

Her thoughts were interrupted as a Crow warrior seized her by her waist. He lifted her from her feet and began to make his way towards the tree line.

Using the strength of a woman empowered by fear she began to kick and scream... scratching at the wet arms that held her in an iron grip. His clasp tightened around her... threatening to force the air from her. Her breathing became dangerously shallow. Again she tried desperately to break free of the dominating clutches that held her... but her efforts were in vain. With the force of his grip... she could hear the rushing pulse of her own blood in her inner ear... a pulse that had become rapid and erratic.

From nearby she heard the war-cry of Left-Wing... quickly followed by a victory whoop. She tried to call out to him... but she had difficulties finding her breath in the man's grip.

Slowly the Crow's arms begin to loosen... and soon she found herself falling to the soggy ground. She laid there in the mud... sucking in the cool air in loud and wheezing gulps... then exhaling in agonizing sobs.

Above her stood a grinning Left-Wing. She watched as Left-Wing reached down towards the Crow who held her captive. He flipped him over then went to retrieve the tomahawk that was lodged deep in his back. The stone blade was embedded so deeply into his back that he had to put a barefoot on the Crow's back in order to pry it loose using both hands.

"White-Sun!" Left-Wing called out.

The Deer-Lady's wet hair was plastered to her face and shoulders. With a hand caked with mud, she wiped the back of her hand over her forehead to clear her hair from her eyes. Blinking against the rain she saw as White-Sun approached Left-Wing. He said something to her above the noise of the rain... then the woman came to help her to her feet.

More war cries... more lightning... more thunder... more bloodshed... it was all too overwhelming for the Deer-Lady. She could feel the anger and hatred of the warring warriors scalding her heart. She tried turning off her senses... blocking out the hate... the bloodlust... but the unimaginable violence was more than she could block out.

"We have to go!" White-Sun shouted above the chaos. The two then raced towards the forest to escape detection... but a Crow had spotted them.

From across the clearing Red-River spotted the two women as they entered the tree line. He knew they were women for only they would flee in the heat of battle. The love of battle was a notorious characteristic trait amongst the Lakota. For to them... the battleground is a place to prove courage and bravery... a place to enter the realm of manhood.

Instinctively he knew one of them had to be Bull's-Tail. So with weapons in hand, he went to cross the clearing... moving through grass that was made slick with rain. To his left, a Lakota warrior made himself visible. He approached Red-River and a low crouch. In his hand, he held a flint knife... there was no fear on his face... but instead a look of wild and raw anger. His face was plastered with mud and oozing blood. His long hair was parted down the middle with tightly woven braids hanging wetly over each shoulder... these braids were plastered to his heaving chest. On his lips danced a wolfish grin that could be seen even in the darkness... his teeth were red with blood... his eyes smoldering with hatred.

Red-River took a hesitant step backward... which only invoked the Lakota's wrath. He repositioned his own weapon in hand... tightening his grip... allowing the weight of the weapon to rebalance itself. At that moment the Lakota launched forward... his knife slicing through the wet air.

The Crow leader lifted his own weapon high above his head. This action caused his still wounded abdomen to scream out in agonizing pain. A pain he had to push aside for now... for he needed to mustard all the strength he could gather in his blow... for his very life may hang in the balance.

As he brought down his Tomahawk the Lakota's knife tore at the flesh of Red-River... ripping the flesh of his side. His own weapon landed heavily with a sickening slap across the Lakota skull. It was a blow that reverberated through the tomahawks handle, up his arm, to the very depths of his being.

As the Lakota slumped over in death... Red-River couldn't help but to grimace at the pain... the pain of both his existing wounds and his newly-acquired injury. He touched the wound delicately... probing at the knife wound... the rain feeling like liquid fire as he felt on the injury.

He applied pressure with a quivering hand... waiting for it to numb itself so he could go after Bull's-Tail. His eyes scanned the battlefield... dreadfully anticipating another attack. He saw that most of the fighting had decreased into small skirmishes here and there. Most of the Little-Star-Band laid either dead or dying on the muddy battlefield. Although his Crow and her allies severely outnumbered the Lakota... the dead or dying Crow seem to vastly outnumber the fallen enemy.

The tragic inevitability of war with this particular tribe, he solemnly thought to himself.

Red-River raise a hand to his face... although it was covered in blood, he felt the throb of his wounds slowly subside... being replaced by the welcoming numbness. Again he looked around himself. He knew the death of his enemies could be rendered more slowly and painfully. And perhaps he would have enjoyed it if he had the time. But he came for one thing.

"Black-Feather!" he called out to one of his Crow warriors. The man quickly approached Red-River. "I saw Bull's-Tail and another woman escaped into the forest," he said as he pointed to the place of which the two had disappeared. "Bring her to me, alive," he ordered. The one called Black-Feather said nothing... instead he turned and took off in a dead sprint... eager to fulfill Red-River's order.

White-Sun and the Deer-Lady dashed into the forest swiftly... branches whipping at their face... stinging in the cold rain. White-Sun pulled the Deer-Lady by her hand... leading the way to safety. And soon the two could no longer hear the battle cries of all-out war behind them. Instead... despite the rain... they found themselves in an eerie silence. Even the rain began to let up.

Even so... the wet closeness of the lush forest seemed to make the early morning even more oppressive.

"White-Sun," whispered of voice from out of the shadows... a voice belonging to Mocking-Bird. They found her crouching under the heavy growth of a bush... and there the three had gathered in the shadows of the lush plant life. Drenched by the night's cold rain... the three sought warmth from each other as they huddled together... inhaling the animal odors of wet buckskin.

A wisp of the Deer-Lady's warm breath met the cool air of the night... sending before her a thick cloud of steam. Her heart continued to hammer against her ribcage with such force that she couldn't stop herself from trembling. She fought desperately to calm herself. She felt White-Sun as her arms wrapped tightly around her.

At that moment... a strange sound caught her ears. She held her breath to listen... but all she could hear was the pulsing rush of blood in her ears. Reluctantly, she opened her senses... painfully taking in the forest. And there... on the battlefield... she heard of them... all of them... both Crow and Lakota... crying out to the Great-Spirit in pain and agony. Calling out to other fallen brothers with desperate hearts. Wordlessly calling out for help... to be saved from the brutal pain their mortal enemies had inflicted upon them.

The Deer-Lady began to weep. She could not help them... she could not save the hurt and falling... she couldn't even save the one who had saved her... Tall-Eagle.

She wept even harder... her tears mixing with a rain and mud on her face. She felt White-Sun's arms embrace her harder... but it was of no comfort. The hurt and pain of the battlefield had cut to her heart like a flint knife... and felt like ice as it pierced her soul. She felt absolute pain... absolute terror. She felt a primal need to rush to their aid... but knew she couldn't. Besides... the pain and hurt of the battlefield was far too great for her weakness. She had to make it stop.

Just as she was about to close herself off from her surroundings... she sensed some unknown presents in the forest. An evil and wicked presents. A rising terror gripped her very soul as she felt countless Crows entering the tree-line to find them.

"They are coming for us," she said as she fought to remain calm. "They are coming for me," she whispered... softly correcting herself. There was no need to inject fear into her words... for the fear darkened her very eyes and soul.

"We are safe here," White-Sun said softly knowing her words were lost to the Mayan. "We shall remain here until the rising of the sun. Or until Left-Wing comes for us."

"Your People are no more," the Deer-Lady solemnly stated in her own language as she broke their embrace. "Your people have fallen. Only the Crow remain," she whispered as she fought back the welling tears. She knew White-Sun didn't understand her words, but she felt them with her soul.

She watched as White-Sun's soft demeanor turned to stone. And in the Lakota language she spat acidly "You brought death to our people." As she spoke... the words and tone she used when she spoke was dispassionate.

The Deer-Lady flinched at the sting of her bitter tone... her lower lip quivering as tears fell freely down her cheeks. "I-I-I'm s-sorry," she softly spattered. "I-I..."

"Are you the seed of the Invaders?" White-Sun asked... knowing the Mayan wouldn't understand. "You are too pale to be of the indigenous people. Too pale to be of the Mayan as you claim. Are you there seed? Their offspring?" she demanded as she glared icily at the Deer-Lady. But the Deer-Lady could say nothing... only stare at the in disbelief.

The rain had stopped completely... and thick clouds in the heavens begin to lighten... turning to a dull gray... evidence of the encroaching dawn.

"Leave us," White-Sun hissed as she shoved the Deer-Lady. She stumbled from their place of concealment... her hands landing in thick mud.

The Deer-Lady looked up at White-Sun with eyes filled with a wild look of desperation. The Deer-Lady parted her lips to protest... but the icy gleam in the eyes of White-Sun discouraged her. She knew her protest would be to no avail. Through bitter experience... she had long ago discovered that nothing is more corrosive or distracted to the human spirit, ethics, or decency then that of the savages of warfare.

But quickly her attention was drawn towards the ensuing Crow. Again she could feel the evilness of their intent.

Again the Deer-Lady looked at White-Sun and Mocking-Bird... her eyes pleading silently with them to run. But White-Sun shooed her off like an unwanted coyote. Full of hurt... the Deer-Lady got to her feet and melted into the surrounding darkness.

White-Sun felt a twinge of sadness deep within her soul. The Deer-Lady had looked so sad... so vulnerable... so lost and alone. No wonder Tall-Eagle felt deeply obliged to protect her... to keep her.

Red-River had ordered more Crow into the forest... their orders were to retrieve Bull's-Tail. Another Crow bandaged Red-Rivers new wound... using long strips of deer hide. He grimaced against the pain as the bandage was pulled tightly.

From the clearing, Red-River was able to clearly see the heavens above. He could tell by the dull colors of the clouds that soon dawn would be upon them. Already the eastern sky was etched with the very first faint traces of a gloomy gray.

Again he looked over the battlefield... the sour stench of blood was heavy on the damp air. He felt his face harden into a gleeful grimace as he surveyed the destruction that laid before him. But for now... he only wanted Bull's-Tail. With this resolve... he followed his men into the forest with this single goal in mind.

Black-Feather crept through the wet brush in search of Bull's-Tail... his eyes unblinking... his every sense sharpened to a point... using all the stuff he had been taught as a child when stalking prey. He had to step softly... for the mud oozing from his moccasins would produce a sucking noise... possibly revealing his position. Despite the coolness of the night... the wetness of rain on his skin was replaced by clammy sweat. He knew that soon his core temperature will plummet... and the wet flesh exposed to the cold air would sap any remaining heat and energy within. So he knew he needed to find the women quickly... or sacrifice stealth for heat by moving quickly.

He knew other Crow scouts had joined the search... for he could hear them hollering and whooping. Such tactics were often used to hunt game in their ancestral Homeland. Some would creep silently while others would create a disturbance to cause a state of panic and confusion within the hunted... driving them from their place of concealment in a mad dash for safety. He began to wonder if such tactics would work on intelligent human beings as well.

In a very low crouch... Black-Feather continued to creep through the forest... his well-honed eyes steadily checking his immediate surroundings for any type of disturbances. Disturbances that held evidence of a human presents. Although the darkness of the eerie morning made it difficult... it didn't make it impossible. For soon he came across the handprints in the mud... left by the Deer-Lady in her hasty departure.

Black-Feather dropped to one knee and slowly ran a hand along the contours of the handprint. He knew it was made recently... very recently... or else the rain would have dulled its sharpness.

He looked around and saw to his immediate left an oak tree... its enormous trunk was cluttered by a moss-covered brush with heavy clumps of foliage. And upon closer inspection, he could tell that it could be hollow.

With his tomahawk he slowly parted the brush. And there... within the plush foliage... he saw the two women.

When their eyes met, Black-Feather smiled derisively... then stood fully erect with supreme arrogance. Even in the closed darkness he could see the frightened face of the younger woman. In fear, she try cowering away behind the older woman... trying to move even further into the shadows of the closed space.

Behind him, he could still hear the whooping and hollering of his Crow brethren. Again he smiled... but abruptly his face darken when he realized that Bull's-Tail wasn't present.

The Crow savagely gripped the older of the two by her hair and pulled her out into the open. The Woman made no attempt at resisting. "Where is the stranger!" he demanded viciously as he slung her head from side to side by her hair.

Looking into the woman's eyes, Black-Feather became frustrated. For if the woman was afraid... she didn't show it. Instead... the Crow found himself staring at a face hardened by hatred and defiance. "All of your men are dead. Do you want to join them in the Land-of-Spirits?" he spat angrily as he pulled her head back viciously by her hair so that she would be looking up at him. But there was no fear in the woman's eyes. And he was aware that if a person wasn't afraid of death... it was of no avail to threaten them.

At that very moment, the second woman sprang from her hiding spot, crashing into him. The unexpected and sudden impact sent Black-Feathers sprawling to the ground... his weapon went sailing from his hand. Taking advantage of the situation, the younger woman helped a second to her feet and the two made a dash for freedom.

His impact with the ground had driven the wind from his chest... which invoked a spirit of raw anger. Now filled with this frustration he got to his feet... snatched his weapon up from the ground and pursued the fleeing women.

As Black-Feather gave chase, he let out a distinctive shrill war-whoop. A war-whoop that told the other Crow he has spotted their target. In response, the war party began to close in on their position... still whooping and hollering as they ran.

It didn't take long for the Crow to encircle the running women. Filled with wild and desperate hope, the two tried fighting through the closing circle of Crow scouts... but their energy was no match for the Crow's brute strength and power. The two were thrown to the muddy ground and a tight circle was formed around them... the faces of the men were stern and keen... almost an eagerness for more bloodshed.

But they didn't make a move.

The two women laid helplessly in the center of the circle... gasping for air. The younger woman's breathe whistled deep in her throat from the exertion of such a hard run. They were covered in mud and filth... their deerskin dresses ragged and tattered.

Black-Feather pushed his way into the circle and stood before the two women... his eyes flickering with anger. He tightened his grip around the handle of his tomahawk. "Are you ready to join your people, woman?!" he spat angrily at the older woman. But the woman said nothing. "If you wish to live, just tell me where the stranger is."

He was met with silence.

Black-Feather turned his attention towards the younger of the two. And there he could read the truth in her eyes... she was afraid... very afraid. She had managed not to cry out... but instead... kept her frightened whispers subdued to the softest of whimpers.

His eyes peered icily at the frightened woman as he approached her... an evil grin playing on his lips.

"Soon you will die for this, Crow," the older woman said with iron resolve.

"Then I may see you in the Land-of-the-Spirits," he responded. And as he spoke... his words were filled with such arrogance and mockery.

"The spirit world is not a place for cowards, Crow," she said... summoning her last bit of defiance.

"So the mighty Lakota fell by the hands of cowards?" His face looked petulant and annoyed.

"Like a mighty Oak tree falling from termites, from insects."

At the statement... Black-Feather lashed out with great fury with his weapon. With a sickening thud it found its mark on the side of the woman's head. The violent blow snapped her head sideways and she fell to the ground... instantly dead.

He then turn his attention back towards the second woman... her young face alight in horror and consternation. "She is dead because she was struck by a feeling of ancestral Pride. Tell me, are you prideful as well?" he said as he squatted next to her.

Fear had been her overriding emotion... not pride. A type of fear that prevented her from responding. "Where is she, Lakota woman?" he asked as he reached out a hand and remove a strand of hair from her face. "How many lives is this stranger worth?"

The woman felt transfixed by her tormentor's terrible gaze. Slowly... a hazy veil of tears began to blur her vision. "White-Sun chased her off," she whispered softly in a voice full of fear and pain. "White-Sun never liked her. Simply tolerated her; nothing more."

"Which way did she run?" he asked.

"I don't know."

"You don't know, huh? So what good are you to me alive?" Every word that he spoke seemed to be uttered with a slight bemused and mock-ish tone.

The woman knew her time had to come. With tears falling freely from her eyes... she cast her gaze upon the heavens... where giant billowy clouds seem to raise the summit of the tall treetops. Everything about her seemed to be merged in a grayish mist ... creating a dreamlike quality to everything.

Perhaps this is what the Land-of-the-Spirits is like? she thought to herself. Then she prepared herself for the journey by singing the Lakota song of the Soul's Journey......

"Look beyond the night... to the Rising Sun.
"Fear not my child... the journey has begun... the journey has begun."

Her voice was soft and low... filled with such beauty and sorrow. And as she sung... her voice grew in power and conviction.

"Ascend through the murky mist... the pain will not last.
"The days of sorrow... has now come to pass.
"Tread the sacred path... our ancestors laid.
"Use the Morning Star... to guide your way.
"To a Mystic place... where peace can be found.
"And soon you will be... upon my sacred ground... upon sacred ground."

Dawn had come upon the Great-Plains. Far to the east, the heavens seemed to glimmer... while a gray light slowly grew about the bloody forest. Tall-Eagle awakening to a searing pain in his head... his tense muscles screamed with pain. The world about him continue to spin dizzyingly as he tried to bring his eyes into focus. His head throbbed in time with his heartbeat. He tried squeezing his eyes shut against the pain... but the darkness of unconsciousness threatened to consume him.

Wicked dreams and evil half-waking had haunted him throughout the early morning hours. Even now he wondered if he was truly among the living... or have found his place in the Land-of-the-Spirits. The pain had veiled the distinction between reality and the dream world... eroding the thin boundaries of a dreadful fact or a painful fantasy.

But the agonizing pain of reality made it all too real.

Before slipping back into one of those evil dreams he forced his eyes open. Slowly... as if recovering from a terrifying dream he began to recall what took place. He reached a trembling hand to his head and flinched at the pain. Although he couldn't fully recall every detail... he knew he suffered a terrible head injury, for his hair was thickly matted with blood.

Again he tried to bring his eyes into focus... his entire body felt as if it was fully emerged in liquid fire. Slowly he crawled to his knees.

Although rain had fallen the night before... he could see his body was covered with insect bites ... for where there wasn't mud there was swollenness and tiny specks of blood. Even from these tiny injuries he could feel the sensation of fiery needles biting into his flesh.

For an instant he wanted to lay back down... never to rise again. For an instant, he became eager to join his ancestors and a place of no tears... a place of no fear... a place of no pain. But only for a brief instant... for then his mind turn towards the Deer-Lady. And it was at this very moment... he knew he had to get up.

Tall-Eagle had come to love this woman more and more with each passing day. With the rising of each sun she had become more and more apart of him. Even now... as he lay at the very hands of pain and misery... even now as he lay just this side of the grave... he thinks not of himself or the welfare of his people. Instead, he thinks only of her. Everything else in the natural world had become secondary to this warrior.

Painfully he got to his feet. The world swam about him in a dizzying manner as he fought to maintain his balance. Again his hand reached for his wounded head... and again he flinched at the pain.

Slowly he began to make his way through the woods... stumbling with each step. He was heading in the direction of the campsite when he spotted the body of Leaping-Fox. Immediately his heart sank for he knew instantly that Leaping-Fox was unable to deliver his warning to the Little-Star-Band. Which meant that the Deer-Lady could be in danger.

His heart sank as the threat of Red-River echoed through the tortured abyss of his mind. The threat to cause her harm. And the mere thought of such innocent beauty so dreadfully endangered filled him with rage and hatred. He felt hot tears welling up behind his eyes... but the warrior within refuse to let them fall.

Tall-Eagle went to where Leaping-Fox laid... a single spear protruding from his breastplate... his entire chest was black with dry blood... evidence that he suffered the injury throughout the night. Or at least until the rain has stopped falling. His face of death looked painfully tense... as if death had brought him no peace.

His heart went out to his fallen brother, Leaping-Fox. *How fragile life is,* he thought to himself. Leaping-Fox had only witnessed the passing of twenty winters... but now he lay dead. In the scope of eternity... life seems to pass through the light all too quickly. He wanted desperately to mourn for his brother... to perform the proper Ceremonies for his passage. But Tall-Eagle had neither the strength nor energy to perform such duties. And again... his thoughts turn towards the Deer-Lady.

Fire burned in the chest of the Deer-Lady as she ran with all her might. She had lost her moccasins long ago and the mud was heavy and thick on her feet. Her heart... wildly pumping within the confines of her chest... her lungs pushing against her ribs. But despite the brutal strain on her slender body... she continued to run as hard as she could.

A lot of the forest still lay dark and dim... completely untouched by the light of dawn. The rain had diminished long ago... but there was a heavy mist in the air... a big cloud of oblique fog... as if the rain of the night refused to relinquish its hold. In her mind, she imagine the sounds of feet in pursuit... breaking the silence of the dawn. So terrified was she that she thought she heard the footfalls floating towards her on the liquid air. It drove her to run harder.

She ran until she could run no more. When she stopped she use a tree to keep herself from falling. Sweat poured from her body... her hand trembling as she held the tree. Her deerskin dress was plastered to her shaking body... cold and slick against her burning flesh.

Slowly she allowed herself to drop to her knees on the wet and soggy ground. She rested her face against the trunk of a tree... allowing the coolness to draw the heat from her forehead. Above her she heard the non-stop chattering of scrambling squirrels and the singing of birds. She looked up to see soft leaves quivering on the gentle breeze... reflecting the light of the heavens.

After she slowed her breathing... she turned around and braced her back against the tree. There she sat silently... listening to the voices of the forest... dreading to hear sounds of a chase.

There was none. There was only the natural sounds of the forest. And a sense of sheer emptiness seemed to encircle her. A sense of emptiness and aloneness.

Knowing she needed to keep moving, she slowly got to her feet. Part of her wanted to open herself up... or if anything to see if she was being pursued. But the emotional toll her last encounter brought upon her cause her spirit to quiver with cold dread.

But fear was offset by hope. The hope of feeling the warm presence of Tall-Eagle. But her tortured mind drifted to the thought she had earlier. Thoughts of how the warrior Tall-Eagle would never allow an enemy party to launch a sneak-attack upon his People... not while there was still life within him.

Again her heart begins to ache and tears began to flow... as if aware by emotional instinct that she would never lay eyes upon Tall-Eagle again. At the painful realization, she stumbled and fell to her knees... her very heart had been jarred from her body. She let out a low... mournful cry as she placed her head into her hands.

You will be safe with me, she recalled him saying to her... his first words to her in a time that seemed so long ago. An eternity. But now... these whispered words begin to echo loudly in the depths of her heart... in the depths of her soul. Again she cried out in pain... both physical and emotional. She wanted to call out his name... but the only sound she could manage was the softest of moans.

But she needed to survive. She needed to get as far as she could away from the Crow... for she knew that acid venom of vengeance would be scolding the black heart of Red-River... her death would be rendered slowly and painfully... but she knew from bitter experience that the Crow had a repulsive taste for brutality.

So again she got to her feet... slowly... but steadily. The sadness of her soul and the emptiness of her heart had blended into a tunnel of pure misery. A misery that seemed to increase with every step she made away from The Little-Star-Band camp... with every step she made away from where Tall-Eagle laid.

"Safe journey," she whispered softly... in a voice that went out to the peaceful heart of the forest.

Then she started to walk... but a strange sound caught her ear... a soft rustling just behind her. Her heart began to pound as her breathing quicken. She stopped short to listen... all senses on full alert... but the sound has stopped as well. Doing all she could to control the panic that soared through her, she turned to face the possible dangers that lay behind her... ready to face it head on.

The trek for Tall-Eagle was long and strenuous... his body still ached and his head continued to throb... but finally he arrived at the campsite... lights of the heavens reach down into the clearing... gently touching the wet and blood-soaked battlefield. The foul stench of the dead and the dying attracted the attention of vultures who circled slowly overhead. A bold vulture had even landed in the midst of the bloody aftermath... with it's enormous wings spread out, it was hopping on it's thin legs towards the body of a fallen Lakota warrior.

Tall-Eagle watched in horrified fascination as it's razor-sharp talons dug deep trenches into his naked skin... then begin to feast upon the torn flesh. In anger, he stumbled after the vulture... yelling with all his might as he went... interrupting its unholy repressed. The vulture let out a low screech then immediately took flight... rejoining the other scavengers on a celestial current of the heavens

A soft stirring of a Lakota had caught his attention... and a dark shadow crept over his heart as he found himself looking at his closest friend... Left-Wing.

As he approached Left-Wing he saw two jagged ends of bone had torn through the skin of his chest... glistening a dull white as dark blood welled up around it. His breathing was raspy as he struggled to inhale. Unyielding pain and grief raged through him as he crouched over his friend.

Left-Wing managed to open his eyes... but was unable to focus them. Still struggling to breathe... he whispered "Tall-Eagle, my brother." Then he began to laugh... and with great effort he said "I thought you were the Spirit-of-Death. And it made me question, why could Death not send a beautiful woman?"

It was often this black humor that had been Tall-Eagle saving grace... even now it brought a grim smile to his lips.

"I am not death, my friend. But it seems he is on the prowl," Tall-Eagle agreed somberly.

Left-Wing coughed again... and for the briefest moment... a flicker of pain flashed across his face. "I am ready for him... rest assured, my brother... Death would not take me alive."

Tall-Eagle smiled again. But it was a weary, detached smile of a man who has lost too much too fast. And then he found himself blinking against the bitter sting of unshed tears. He forced himself to look away... but everywhere his eyes fell... it fell upon death and destruction.

Just off to his left lay the body of Brave-Shield... another great warrior. His bloody carcass was riddled with stab wounds... proof that he fought until he could fight no more. Just beyond him were two Crow warriors... laying in twin pools of their own blood. And just beyond them was the Lakota warrior Pretty-Elk, whose tomahawk lay mere inches from his outstretched fingertips. And that's when he noticed other movement within the clearing... other survivors... both Lakota and Crow... barely clenching onto life. There were even a few Lakota warriors sitting up... nursing their bloody wounds.

"How many have fallen?" Left-Wing asked as he tried to look around.

Tall-Eagle couldn't answer immediately. He had to wait for the turmoil within to subside. "Too many," he said finally as he turned back towards his friend. "Too many," he repeated softly as he watched the dark blood as it ran freely from Left-Wing wounds. He knew the injury was getting worse due to him talking. "Lay quiet, my friend."

"To what end? So that my life can be spared?" he asked stubbornly. "My time has come. I can feel my spirit seeping through my chest." Again he coughed, and his dry lips was forming more words... but there was not a trace of an audible sound.

A stricken look crossed the face of Tall-Eagle... but it was quickly masked... for the warrior that lay dying before him deserved a warrior by his side as he exhaled for the very last time. "Are we not Lakota?" he asked his dying friend. "Are we not members of The Little-Star-Band? The most fearless band of the Sioux? And are we not the Warriors of the Wounde-Shield-Society? A society comprised of the fiercest warriors?"

And then Tall-Eagle began to sing the Warrior's song of death... a song reserved only for those brave ones who has fallen on the battlefield. And when he had finished... the spirit of his friend Left-Wing had crossed over to the realm of their ancestors.

Tall-Eagle looked upon the battlefield once more... looking upon the dead and the dying... upon those tortured and dark souls seeking to set free the twisted and dark demons of pain so that their spirits may fly free.

Just before him, he saw movements. Instantly he knew it was a wounded warrior who laid just below a tree. But he could tell it wasn't Lakota nor Crow. But if it wasn't either or... then who was it?

Instantly, Tall-Eagle was upon him... seizing him roughly by his beaded breastplate... pulling him into a sitting position against the tree. The man was breathing hoarsely... his eyelids fluttering and his eyes roll to the back so that only the whites of his eyes showed. Tall-Eagle could tell the man was in great pain. But it did little to relieve the boiling anger and hatred he had raging within... boiling anger and hatred for those who had committed such a brutal atrocity upon his people.

"Who are you?" he snarled waspishly... grabbing the man's jaw in his hand. Again his eyeballs rolled to the back of his head. Little specks of spittle and bubbles of blood formed on his pasty-dry lips. "Who are you?" Tall-Eagle repeated forcefully. He then looked over the injured man and found the source of his pain.

On his side, just below his breastplate was fresh meat which glistened dully in the morning light... the results of being speared... deeply. With the way Lakota weapons were fashioned... the head of a spear can easily be inserted into human flesh... but its jagged underside rips and tears the flesh as it's extracted. As a result... the more meat around the wound... the deeper the thrust.

"I am Arikara," he whispered softly... yet proudly. Again the hatred began to burn him from within as the acid-like adrenaline worked its way through his veins. The Arikara was an enemy of the Sioux. They were a small tribe who were once defeated by the Sioux in a fight over hunting grounds. Legend has it that their numbers had been so greatly reduced that their numbers had never fully recovered. And this was in a time long before the birth of his father's father.

Again the threats of Red-River echoed in his mind... how the Crow would have gathered their allies and wipe the Lakota from this earth. *But weren't the Arikara and Crow enemies?* Again Tall-Eagle took the Arikara jaw in an iron grip. "Why are you here?"

With great difficulties, the dying man said how messenger/scouts of Red-River had come to his People... offering a temporary truce with the Arikaras so that they may go to war together against the Sioux. The messenger/scout also explained how other tribes... other enemies of the Sioux will also join the ranks to ensure victory. After much discussion, the chiefs of the Arikaras thought it wise for them to fight together against a common enemy... necessary to both soften their numbers and to avenge the blood of their ancestors a mere three generations ago. And more importantly to reclaim the ancestral homelands that were stolen from them.

Tall-Eagle was so engrossed in the Arikara's words that he hadn't noticed that three wounded Lakota were upon them... listening to the horrid and bleak future that lay before them. It wasn't until the Arikara looked past Tall-Eagle and said "you will all die," did Tall-Eagle know he wasn't alone.

Tall-Eagle looked up to find Yellow-Horse, Dog-Chief, and

Bad-Claw standing above them... each seemed to be covered with drying mud and blood. Bad-Claw seemed to be favoring his left side of his body... for he was constantly moving... shifting his weight to his right foot.

Dog-Chief looked at Tall-Eagle... his expression extremely hostile. Yellow-Horse face was dirty and flushed... but his eyes were filled with the sparkling fires of hatred for the Arikara he had babied ever since he was a child. His grandmother had been brutally murdered by them... and his mother had instilled in him a hatred that left him eager for war against the cowardly Arikara people.

But the young Bad-Claw with the injured leg seemed to be greatly affected by the words of the dying man. Deep within he found himself fervently praying the words spoken by the Arikara wasn't true... but merely an exaggeration to install fear into the Little-Star-Band.

"You will all die," the dying man repeated softly... the threats seemed to force itself painfully from his bloody mouth. "And we shall retrieve what is rightfully ours," he said with a faint note of triumph in his weak voice.

Tall-Eagle stood fully erect. Despite his injuries he still held the air of a man completely in charge. He bent over to grab ahold of the dying man's weapon... a highly-decorated beaded lance, trimmed with animal fur and three bear claws dangling from the handle. He rolled it around in the palm of his hand... feeling the weight and balance of the weapon`.

"How many Lakota lives have you taken with this?" Tall-Eagle ask.

Slowly the Arikara started to laugh... but it was quickly interrupted by a painful cough. "The Creator smiles upon the Lakota, for I was injured before I can put it to use," he said with the hint of an indignant snort.

Such revelations caused Tall-Eagle to chuckle as well. "Say your prayers, Arikara, for soon you will join your ancestors," Tall-Eagle stated as he handed Yellow-Horse decorative lance.

With demented delight, Yellow-Horse took ahold of the weapon and waited for Tall-Eagle to walk away. He then lifted the lance and brought an abrupt end to the slowly dying man.

Behind him... Tall-Eagle heard the wet slap of rock against bone. He shrugged eternally and the strong features of his face settled into a mask of disappointment. *More for the vultures,* he thought grimly to himself.

But looking towards the skies he noticed the absence of these nefarious scavengers. He looked towards the battlefield... expecting to find them feasting upon the bloody ruins of the Little-Star-Band... but they were nowhere to be seen.

There was a little more movement by the survivors... still too many Lakota lay dead. Barely surviving Lakota were being attended by other injured Lakota. Wounded enemy intruders were ignored... they're dying moans were swept up by the gentle winds... drifting over the cold and gray clearing.

"What now?" Yellow-Horse asked as he approached Tall-Eagle from behind... then stood by his side.

"Our paths must diverge, my friend," Tall-Eagle said without taking his eyes off the field. "You and the others will stay behind to bury our dead. Two scouts must ride forth to the land of the Oglala to seek assistance. And I..." Tall-Eagle tried forming a few fumbling words... but there was the slightest hint of a quiver in his voice... a sort of thickness as his emotions swelled in his chest... threatening to break the surface. So he allowed his sentence to trail off into silence.

"The Deer-Lady," Yellow-Horse said cautiously. Tall-Eagle said nothing. But he didn't need to... for even from Tall-Eagle's profile... Yellow-Horse could see the emptiness and desperation in the depths of his tired eyes. "How do you know she is alive?" he asked the acting chief.

"Who's alive?" Bad-Claw asked as he made his presence known. Trepidation, confusion, and curiosity were warring within his young heart. Curiosity seems to be winning out. "Do you speak of the Deer-Lady?" he finally asked.

"We need to find horses," Yellow-Horse stated... quickly diffusing the situation. "No doubt the Crow and their allies had stolen ours."

"Blue-Stalk is our fastest and he possesses the stealth of a wildcat," Dog-Chief suggested. "He is there," he said pointing towards the battlefield. He was helping Brave-Shield to his feet. "He looks injured. But he is a warrior."

"Indeed he is," Tall-Eagle said. "Blue-Stalk and Big-Scout shall leave at once. Bad-Claw," he called to the youngster. "Tell both Blue-Stalk and Big-Scout they are to travel to the lands of the Oglala in search of help. Tell them to look for horses as they go to assist them. Now go!"

As instructed, Bad-Claw limped to where Blue-Stalk and Brave-Shield stood.

"Leaping-Fox is no more," Tall-Eagle said... much too distracted to pretty things up. "He lies just before our place of concealment. Blue-Leaf know where it is. Take him and bring back the body of Leaping-Fox," he told Dog-Chief

"Blue-Leaf has crossed over as well," Dog-Chief informed Tall-Eagle grimly.

"As did Pretty-Elk, Little-Bull, Big-Nose, Turns-Black, Big-Rock, and many many others, as you can see." As Yellow-Horse said the latter he swept a hand in front of him. "There is but a few left."

"And many gravely injured," Dog-Chief said... echoing the thoughts of both Tall-Eagle and Yellow-Horse

"As I said, I must depart. Yellow-Horse will lead in a ceremony."

"Lead in ceremony?" Yellow-Horse repeated it with a sense of discovery. "But I should join you in your search," he said as his voice simmered with barely suppressed rage. "You know my hatred for them runs deep."

"Of this, I am aware. But our numbers are few and our distance from home is great. At this time, we must be One, my brother. Unity and discipline is our key to survival. Nobody here questions your capabilities in battle... nor your love for your people. Due to this leadership, you can keep them in line, for anything less may let in death," Tall-Eagle said.

What he said was true... but the real reason he wanted to go alone was because he didn't want to be responsible for another Lakota's death. Not at the pursuit of his own happiness... and how could he explain this to a warrior? How could he express the overwhelming burden of guilt that weighs heavily on his guilt-filled heart?

"This is true," Dog-Chief agreed. "No doubt the others will voluntarily be receptive to your leadership," he continued ... almost as a calculated afterthought.

"Now I must go. Dog-Chief, you will find Leaping-Fox at the foot of the hill. Bring him back so that his bones will be with his brothers of war."

Tall-Eagle then went to his own tipi to gather his weapons. He selected his strongest bow... made of hickory and the hardened in the fire of a medicine man's lodge. Normally he wouldn't give much weight to such superstitions, but at this time he felt he needed such luck.

He ran his fingers along the graceful curve of the bowl and then pulled on the taunts sinew string. He then gathered as many arrows as his quiver could hold. Before he exited the lodge... he look back to where the Deer-Lady had laid just the night before. That's where they shared laughs and stories... talking until she could no longer stay awake. A time not too long ago... but a time that felt like an eternity ago.

Again he felt tears gathering in the corners of his eyes. He wiped at them quickly... then sat staring at the wetness that glistened on his fingertips. And as he looked from the wetness to where the Deer-Lady had laid her head... he felt a livid sadness rising up inside of him. He knew that their souls had become inextricably linked... inseparably entwined.

And the memory of her laying in his lodge... the perfect scene etched forever in his mind... had only increase the outpouring of his grief. Bitter tears were stinging his eyes as one fell down his cheek. But then... his sorrow had gave way to anger... for then he thought of Red-River.

As he thought of his mortal enemy he realized this Crow had accomplished what no man could ever do... made Tall-Eagle shed a tear. An urge for vengeance rose up inside of him like molten lava. And he knew the heat of this anger would not only keep him alive but would also push him to succeed. And his vengeance would be so great... so terrible... that legends and songs will be told for generations to come... for his victory will be worthy of such tales.

Outside his lodge he heard Yellow-Horse singing the song for the warriors who have fallen in battle. Soon the voices of others will join in. Their voices were low... full of pain and sadness... in stark contrast with the voice of Yellow-Horse... whose voice was high-pitched and shrill... as the lead singer voice should be.

Although the loss of Left-Wing had greatly darkened his spirit...

Tall-Eagle was thankful for Yellow-Horse, for he knew Yellow-Horse was a leader who could fill a soul devoid of hope with purpose and intent.

With his weapons in hand, Tall-Eagle emerged from his lodge and made his way directly to the tree line without looking back.

Laying before him was a forest where the trees and brush looked as if they were painted with vivid hues of every description... which would make tracking them down a lot easier. He knew what signs to look for... from obvious footprints in the mud to more subtle differences in the coloration of the grass. He knew to look for a bruised stem on a plant... to a change in the direction of overgrown leaves... so the more plant life there is... the easier it is to track. And immediately his eyes went to work

Before he entered he sent his voice to the Great-Spirit... a silent prayer spoken from the heart. And as he prayed he saw the black shape of a giant bird circling overhead. At first he assumed that the bird was a vile vulture... returning to feed off the decaying flesh of his People. But when the mighty bird cried out... it was the unmistakable shrilling screech of an eagle.

For a brief moment his heart softened... for his spirit animal had crept into him... lending him the strength and fortitude he knew he needed in order to fulfill this quest.

Then with a powerful flap of his mighty wings it sped towards the direction of the morning sun. It was only then did he realize where the vultures had gone... despite their numbers, those scavengers would flee at the very sight of such a magnificent bird of prey. *Something closely akin to the Crow and the Lakota*, he thought to himself.

Then he entered the forest.

Many tracks laid before him... all overlapping in a muddy chaos and disarray. But he continued to look until he came across two smaller set of footprints... no doubt the prints belonged to two women. He held back excitement at the discovery... for the pessimism of his wounded heart told him the woman could have easily been White-Sun and Mocking-Bird... for they often stay together. But there was still much hope in his heart... so he continued.

As he walked further into the forest... the beautiful singing of

Yellow-Horse grew fainter and fainter in the growing distance... being replaced by the natural sounds of the wooded area. He listened to the mournful song until at last... it died altogether. And it was then that Tall-Eagle realize... as he stood gazing off into the distance of a small forest... which lies at the heart of an infinite expansion of an evil and unforgiven world... it was then that he realized that... that he was truly alone.

The Deer-Lady's chest was tight with dreadful anticipation as she listened to the oncoming footsteps. Again the bushes shook suddenly... sending an onslaught of burning adrenaline coursing through her veins. Her breathing became dangerously shallow... as her mind raced feverishly.

From beneath the whispering leaves of the brush step of a young fawn. Cautiously... the Deer-Lady slowly relaxed her tense muscles. Slowly she exhaled the pint-up breath she held in her chest and allowed the sudden burst of adrenaline it to subside... slowly flowing out of her like water onto the ground.

The fawn, completely unaware of her surroundings, took another furtive step out of the brush... amateurly taking in it's environment. The Deer-Lady remained motionless as she watched the young fawn lift it's tiny head so that it may eat from the bush.

It was then she began to think of Tall-Eagle and the stories of his childhood... how he had never tired of studying the habits of the creatures who dwelled within the woodlands. She reminisced on the legends of how the Creator thought highly of the Deer-People... so with his brush he lovingly painted the spots on their offspring's body so that they may blend with the shadows of the deep grass and brush.

The Deer-Lady had become so lost in that delicate moment that she didn't see the doe as it crept stealthily out of the bush... stepping so light and so gracefully that it startled it's own young.

The young fawn startled... letting out a little yelp.

The Deer-Lady smiled to herself. The deer have crazy eyes that were so big... so round... so soft. She watched as the doe took a cautious step forward... its large brown eyes surveying the area. The little fawn boldly stepping forth and resumed eating. The doe hesitated... but then stepped out fully from beneath the brush and begin to feed as well.

The Deer-Lady listen to the sound of them nibbling at the leaves... leaves that were dark and polished... leave that gleamed in the light of the climbing sun. They then went to feed on the pines of an evergreen... but the wind must have changed direction for the doe's head shot up... as if it caught her scent upon the breeze.

The doe ominously shifted its large eyes... searching for any signs of danger. The Deer-Lady stood perfectly still. Even so... the doe became so spooked that both she and the young fawn turned and bound away on quick hooves... diving deep into the shadows of the brush... their steps as light as dry leaves on the wind. And again the Deer-Lady found herself alone.

But she had always been alone. Ever since she escaped the war-torn ruins of her accessorial home land... ever since she escaped her forced marriage to a pale-face invader... and every since she's wandered aimlessly through countless lands... being captured and being rescued... and now fleeing for her life... she had always been alone. Wondering strange lands... her very bones aching with the unyielding pain of hard traveling and her heart heavy with loss. But still, she must continue.

Not knowing where she is going... but knowing she could never return to the places she has been... she knew she must continue.

And as she walked through the forest of the plains... she was unaware of the pair of cynical eyes that was watching her every move. A pair of eyes that was seething with bloodlust.

She heard a slight rustling to her right... a moment later a man appeared... his features twisted with resentment and she felt transfixed by his terrible gaze. Then moving like an evil and silent spirit towards her, he covered the distance with rapid speed.

In paralyzing fear... all she could do was whimper as a pair of arms snatched her up off the ground... arms which held her in a vice-like grip... arms that tighten with each breath she exhaled.

Just above her head, she heard the war-cry of her captor. She knew he was notifying the other warriors of their location. She knew that once again she will be surrounded by Crow warriors... Crow warriors that wanted to do her harm. She fought desperately to keep from falling within the realms of unconsciousness. Her vision grew blurry for several seconds. But she fought back unconsciousness. But with the vise-like grip growing even more tighter... all she could do was say a little prayer as she was plunged into darkness.

Tall-Eagle heart dropped when he heard the victory war-cry. All around him were the whooping and hollering of Crow warriors on the hunt. But this particular war-cry... he knew was a signal to the rest that the Deer-Lady had been located.

The forest all about him seemed surreal. A hazy veil of tears began to blur his eyes. He knew he was outnumbered... but he also knew the Deer-Lady life was in peril. He felt helpless. He felt himself as a shadow of his true self... a shadow inhabiting a shadow world.

He tried to regroup mentally... trying to prepare for what he knew he must do. He knew this next fight will be his last. But if he were to cause a diversion... this should give the Deer-Lady just enough time to escape. And this time... with prayers... she will make her way to freedom.

The group of Crow warriors gathered in a small clearing. Black-Feather emerged from the tree line with the unconscious woman slung over his bronze shoulder. He took her to the center where he laid her out for display... as if she was a prized trophy.

Upon contact, the sudden impact jarred the Mayan woman back to life. Panic flared within her as she looked about herself. All around her were leaned faced warriors... all bent with angry and hostile expressions as they collectively stared at her with dark eyes.

There were tears in her own eyes... dampening the dirt and grime below them... leaving little muddy stains on her cheeks.

A few of the warriors eyed her with cruel sexual interest. One of the warriors even attempted to touch her soft downy-like hair... but was quickly reprimanded by another warrior. The two snapped at each other like rabid dogs bearing their teeth.

Suddenly the group shifted... and that is when he appeared... Red-River... slowly walking towards her like a predatory wolf stalking it's helpless prey. The group watched as he approached her and stood over her in all his dark glory. She ominously shifted her soft ebony eyes... looking up at him... feeling every ounce of hope slowly draining from her body.

"Look at all the destruction you have brought," he declared vehemently. "It seems as if wherever you go, death is sure to follow."

His venomous words scraped across her very soul like a jagged knife. In her mind's eyes she saw the destruction of so many people. People that she cared for. People that she loved.

Her head dropped to the soft grass and she began to weep. *Perhaps death is my only chance for vindication.*

"Who do you weep for?" Red-River hissed as he squatted beside her. "Do you weep for the many who have died for you? Do you weep for those who died because of you? Or do you weep for yourself?"

"Please," she whispered ever-so softly. "Please put an end to my story."

"Oh, lost Mayan, who have wandered so far from home, I have no intentions of killing you," Red-River said.

At the statement he could hear angry mumbles of protest from the circle. He then stood up to eye those who surrounded him. In turn they all glared at him with icy stairs. "But it is our law, she must die because of a crime against your brother. It is the only form of retribution," one of the Crow warriors stated.

Realizing his mistake, Red-River grinned slightly, then approached the one who protested his decision. Standing eye to eye, he challenged the warrior with a hostile glare. "Do you think she deserves a quick death? Do you think she deserves such mercy?" Red-River hissed. "This lost Mayan deserves exactly what I have in store for her."

Then with a closed fist he lashed out at the warrior, catching him by surprise and connecting with his jaw. The warrior's head snapped back as he fell to the ground.

The injured Crow stirred in a semiconscious haze. He mumbled something as he reached towards his jaw to baby his injury.

Red-River then turned towards the remainder of the group. "Need I have this conversation with anybody else?"

They remained silent.

"This is good," Red-River said as he turned his attention back towards the weeping Mayan. Truthfully, up until that very moment Red-River had no idea how he was going to get the Mayan out of there alive. Up until that very moment he did not have a plan for sneaking the Mayan away, and then running off with her. But thanks to Crow insolent... he bought himself more than enough time.

"Stand her up," Red-River ordered. Two of the Crow warriors did as instructed, they snatched her to her feet and held her before their leader. "If only you knew," he whispered to the Mayan as he gently touched her soft hair.

Tall-Eagle passed through the forest until he came to a clearing. And in that clearing he saw the gathering of Crow warriors. They all stood in silence, staring towards the center of the crowd. Instantly he knew what they were staring at. His heart dropped at the thought of the Mayan in danger.

Slowly he crept through the bush, trying to find a better place for observation. But there were too many gathered.

He could see the sheer terror in the eyes of the Mayan... and it tore at his wounded heart. Quickly he cuffed his hands around his mouth and let out the soft hoot of an owl. But it was to no avail. Again he tried… this time a little harder… a little louder. But still… he could not alert the Mayan of his presence.

He felt lost and alone, knowing not what to do. But he knew he had to do something. But he what? He possessed no plan, no strategy, no tactic, there was nothing he could do to increase his odds of success.

The Mayan's heart leapt with joyful anticipation when she heard the call of the owl. But she dared not react to it… for doing so would only bring the wrath of the Crow to the hidden Tall-Eagle. *Besides… what could the brave warrior do against so many?* she thought sadly to herself. Even so… she felt comfort in the knowledge that he was near.

It was then he saw as the Mayan was snatched to her feet… being held by two Crow warriors. A sudden surge of adrenaline rushed through the body of Tall-Eagle as he let out a blood-curling cry and leapt from the bush. Driven by peer instinct he rushed towards the group of Crow warriors. He slashed out with his lance and his tomahawk. He felt the sudden resistance of Crow flesh as he slashed away at the group. There were a burst of pain before everything became blurry.

Pain shot through his entire body as he fell to the ground. More pain followed as the Crow warriors quickly overtook him. Consciousness was seeping from him as he heard Red-River above all the commotion.

"Bring him to me!" Red-River demanded.

In his ears Tall-Eagle could hear the ringing and singing of his heavenly ancestors. The taste of blood quickly filled his mouth as he tried peering through swelling eyes. Within mere seconds Tall-Eagle had been beaten beyond recognition.

The Mayan let out a cry as Tall-Eagle was dragged before her. He slumped to the ground in a miserable heap of pain. She managed to escape the grasps of her captors, and then she went to him, kneeling beside him. Afraid to touch him, afraid to cause any more pain, she allowed her hands to hover just above his bruised flesh. Her eyes blurred from a never-ending flow of tears. His painful moans clawed at her heart.

"Awwww... so sad," Red-River mocked as he stood towering above the two. "He thought he could save you. Such wasted bravery. Such foolish bravery."

"Please..." the Mayan said barely above a whisper. But such a plea only enraged Red-River further.

"You plea for this?!?" he rasped. "You plea for this weak one?" He said as he grabbed the Lakota warrior by the hair.

"It is me that you want," the Mayan said. "Let him go, his spirit is true."

"His spirit is mine," Red-River said as he slowly pushed a flint stone knife deep into Tall-Eagle's side.

Tall-Eagle gasped in pain as the cold stone penetrated his hot flesh. Red-River felt Tall-Eagle trembling under his knife.

"Nooooooooooooo!!!!!" the Mayan screamed as she clawed at the face of Red-River.

Driven by peer instinct Red-River withdrew the knife from Tall-Eagle and plunged it into the Mayan. The Mayan gasped as she fell into his arms.

"Noooo," Red-River moan softly. "What did you do?" he asked as he took the Mayan into his powerful arms.

There was confusion amongst the other Crow warriors, but they had disappeared to Red-River. Only this moment mattered to him. Even the slowly dying Lakota warrior became a distant thing. He held the Mayan as he slowly dropped to his knees. He stared into her tear filled eyes as she closed them and exhaled for the very last time.

With her blood on his hand he gently caressed her long wavy hair.

She looked so peaceful... as if asleep. He began to wonder if she had finally found the peace her spirit had longed for... the peace her spirit has yearned for.

Red-River could feel tears welling up in his own eyes. It seems as if all his cunning manipulations were for naught. So lost in this moment that he didn't see nor hear the hundreds of Oglala warriors surrounding the Crow. Nor did he hear Black-Feather as he yelp in fear.

"Red-River!!! It's the Sioux!" Black-Feather cried out.

But it was too late... the Oglala onslaught was fast and brutal. All around Red-River the Crow were falling from arrows and spears... all around Red-River his People were paying for their sins of brutality. All around Red-River came death cries and war-whoops. But Red-River could hear none of it. All he could do was look down upon his shattered dreams of possessing the most beautiful woman he had ever laid eyes upon... the lost Mayan.

EPILOGUE

D ancing-Girl was the first to spot Strong-Spirit, the faithful horse belonging to Tall-Eagle. The Oglala quickly dropped the basket she was using to gather wild berries and ran back to her camp.

Upon reaching her Tribal elder, Appears-Bravely, she told him what she had witnessed. In turn, Appears-Bravely sent scouts to locate the horse, but they needn't travel far for Strong-Spirit had made it's way to the camp. From it's appearance they instantly recognized the horse had survived a brutal encounter. Long, sick gashes oozed blood as the horse danced nervously before them.

"It is Strong-Spirit, the horse belonging to Tall-Eagle of the Little-Star band," Little-Falcon stated.

"They must be in trouble," Appears-Bravely said in a low voice, saying what others were thinking. "Do we know where they went for their hunt?" he inquired.

"Indeed, we do," Kills-Many responded. "They traveled east, along the Folding-Leaf-Path to the lands of Rolling-Hills."

"Prepare the men for war," Appears-Bravely ordered. "And let us pray that we find Tall-Eagle and his People before the angel of death does."